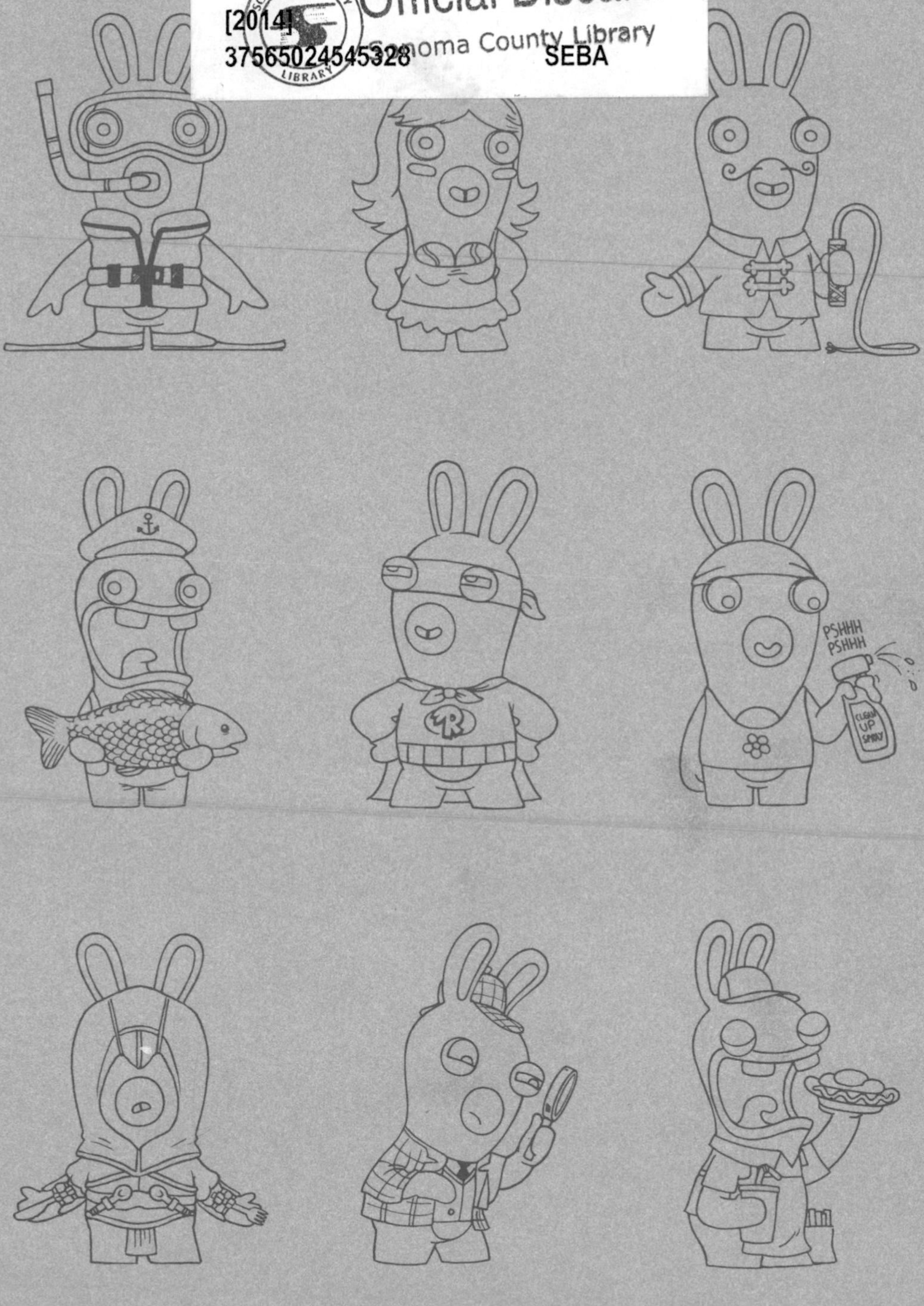
PSHHH
PSHHH
CLEAN UP SPRAY

# #1 "BWAAAAAAAAAAH!"

Thitaume - Writer
Romain Pujol - Artist
Gorobei - Colorist

## PAPERCUTZ™
New York

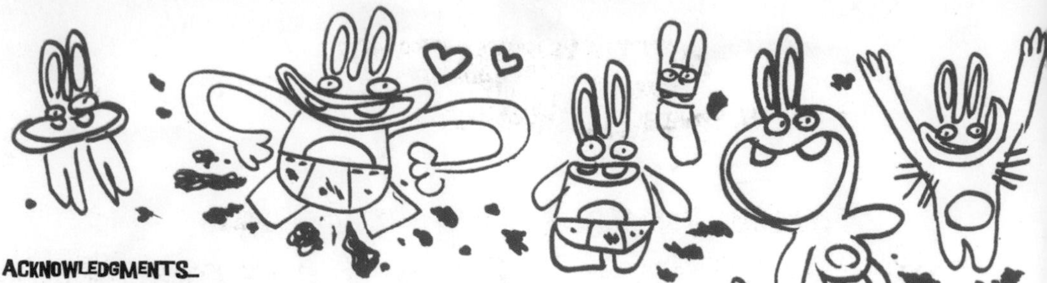

## ACKNOWLEDGMENTS

Thanks to François Tallec for trusting in us and for his oversight throughout the production of this volume.
Thanks also to Cédric Royer for his candidness and his many wise suggestions.
A big thanks to Romain Pujol and Gorobei who, by dint of talent and patience, succeeded in transforming my few ideas into superb comicbook pages.
A special thanks to MAD Fabrik Editions, who let me take my first steps in this profession and especially so to Araceli Cancino for her continued encouragement and helping hand.
Lastly, thanks to Magali for putting up with me on those days when inspiration was wanting.
I dedicate this book to my parents.

*--Thitaume*

Thanks to Thitaume and Gorobei for working enthusiastically along with me to make this book.
Thanks to François Tallec, Cédric Royet and Amy Jenkins for their support through the course of this adventure, as well as to my parents for putting their trust in me.
As for Julie and the readers of my blog, thanks for your patience and commitment.
I'd also like to thank Ubisoft for suggesting to me to rappel down from the heights of their company.
And lastly, I'd like to speak to you, yes, you, who with your sweaty hands are holding this volume, I congratulate you, you have good taste.
I dedicate this book to my family.

*--Romain Pujol*


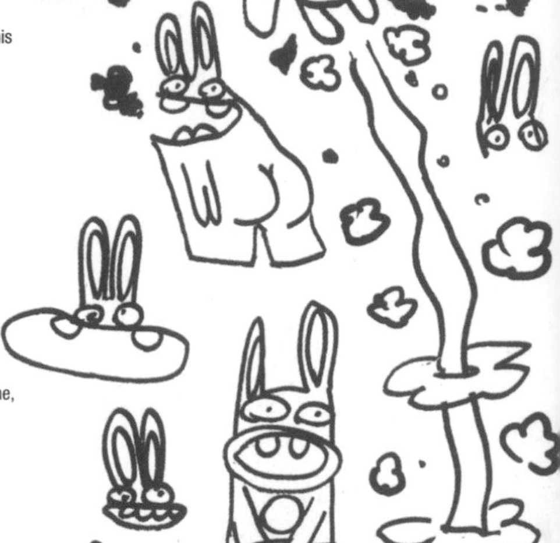


RABBIDS #1 "BWAAAAAAAAAAH!"
Thitaume – Writer
Romain Pujol – Artist
Gorobei – Colorist
Joe Johnson – Translator

978-1-62991-048-2 Paperback Edition
978-1-62991-049-9 Hardcover Edition


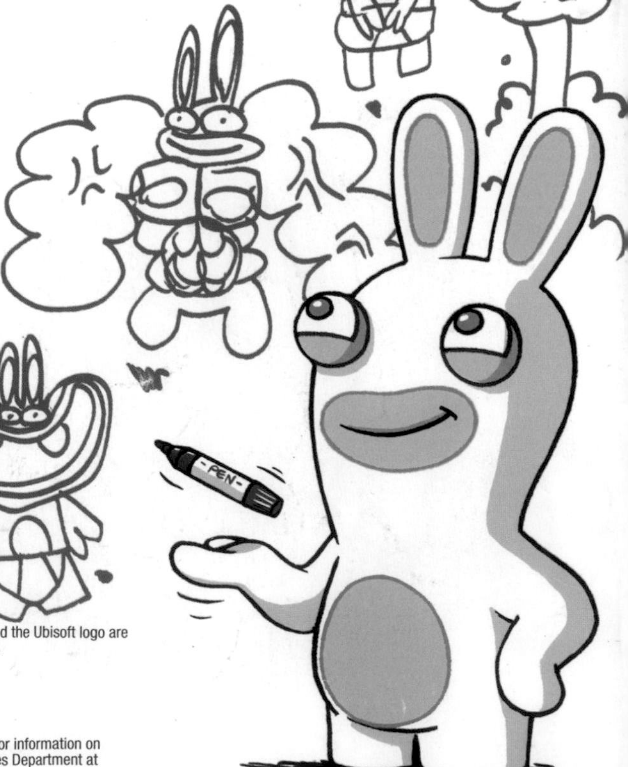
-PEN-

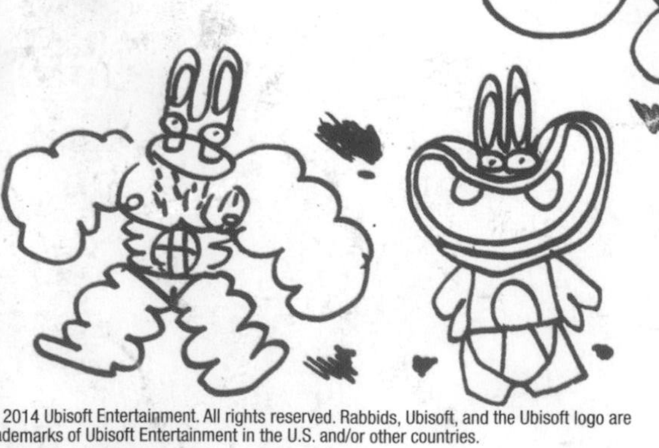




Papercutz books may be purchased for business or promotional use. For information on bulk purchases please contact Macmillan Corporate and Premium Sales Department at (800) 221-7945 x5442.

PRINTED IN THE USA
SEPTEMBER 2014 BY Lifetouch Printing
5126 Forest Hills Ct. , Loves Park, IL 61111

DISTRIBUTED BY MACMILLAN
FIRST PAPERCUTZ PRINTING

# STOP!

You're not at the beginning of the book.
To get there, please follow the directions on page 48.

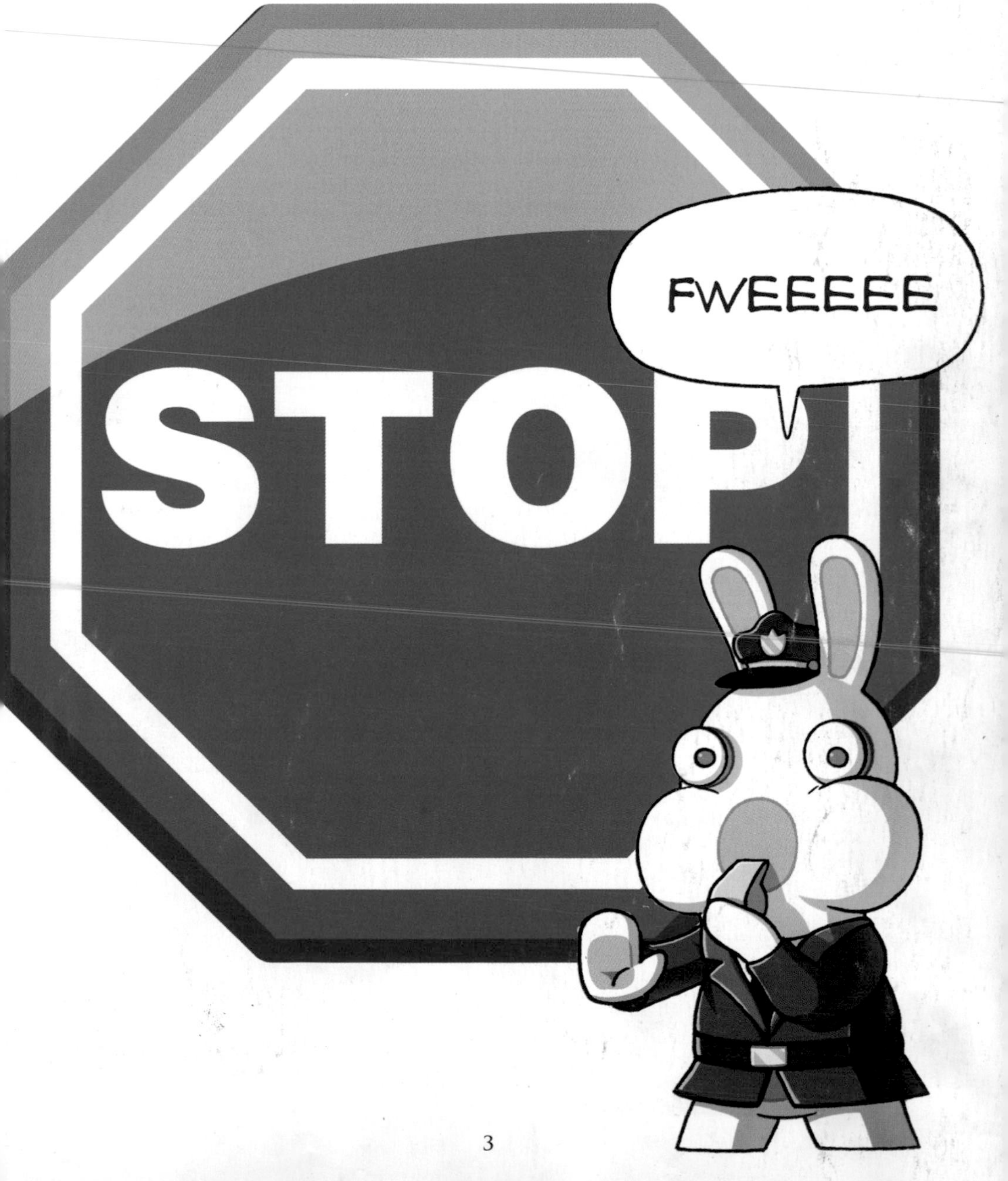
FWEEEEE
STOP

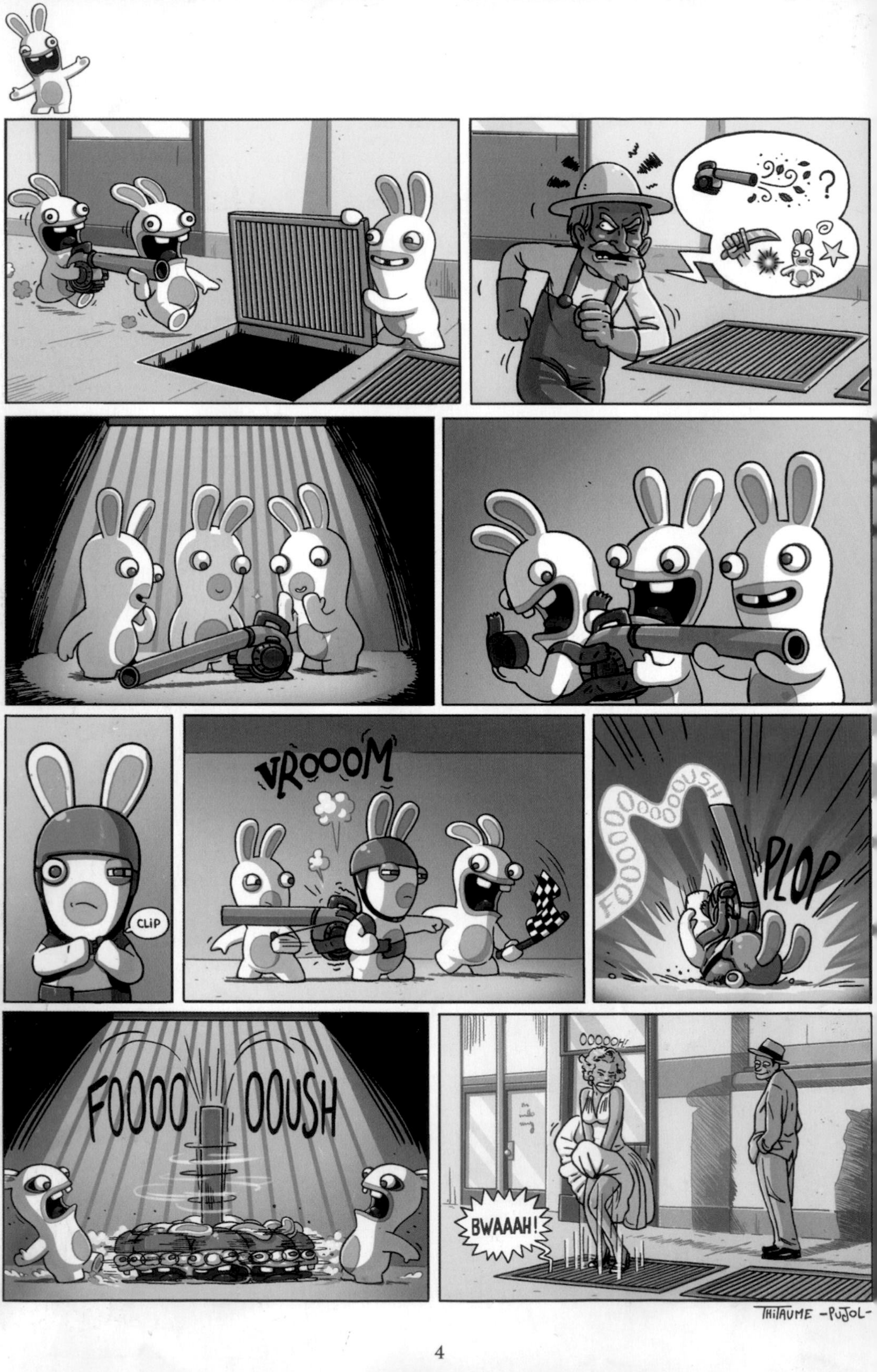
CLIP
VROOOM
FOOOOOOOOOOOOUSH
PLOP
FOOOO OOUSH
OOOOOH!
BWAAAH!
THITAUME -PUJOL-

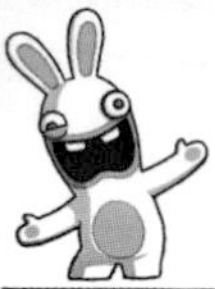

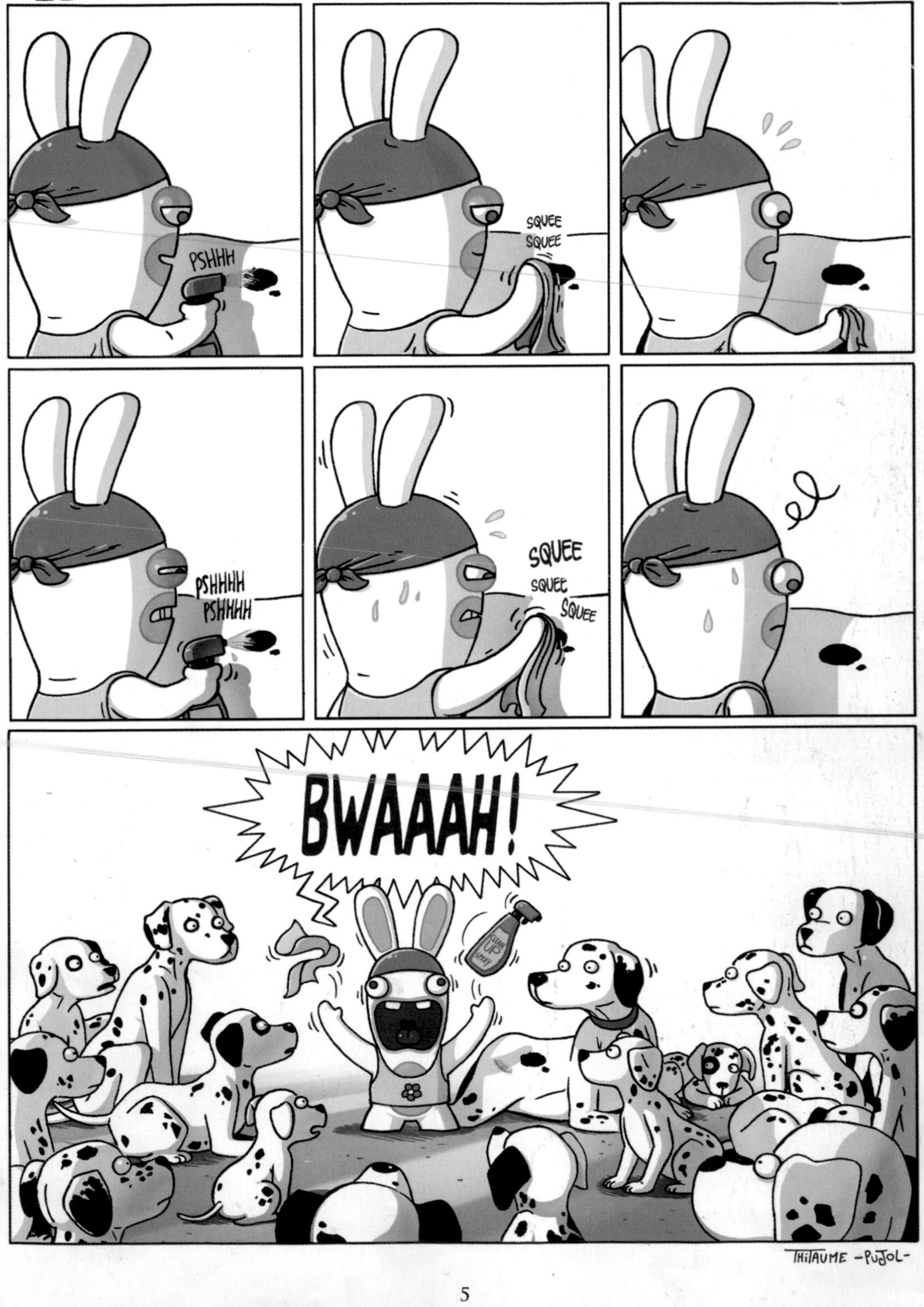
PSHHH
SQUEE
SQUEE
PSHHHH
PSHHHH
SQUEE
SQUEE
SQUEE
BWAAAH!
CLEAN UP SPRAY

THiTAUME -PUJOL-

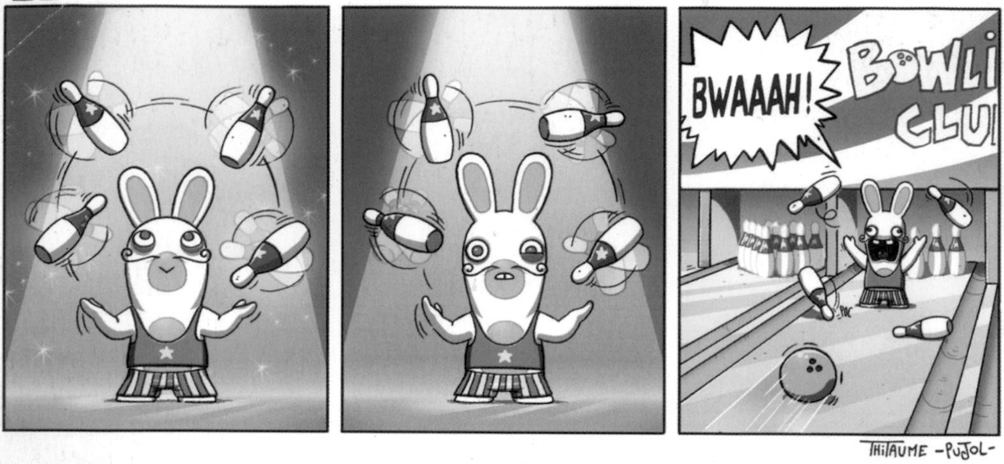
BWAAAH!
THITAUME -PUJOL-

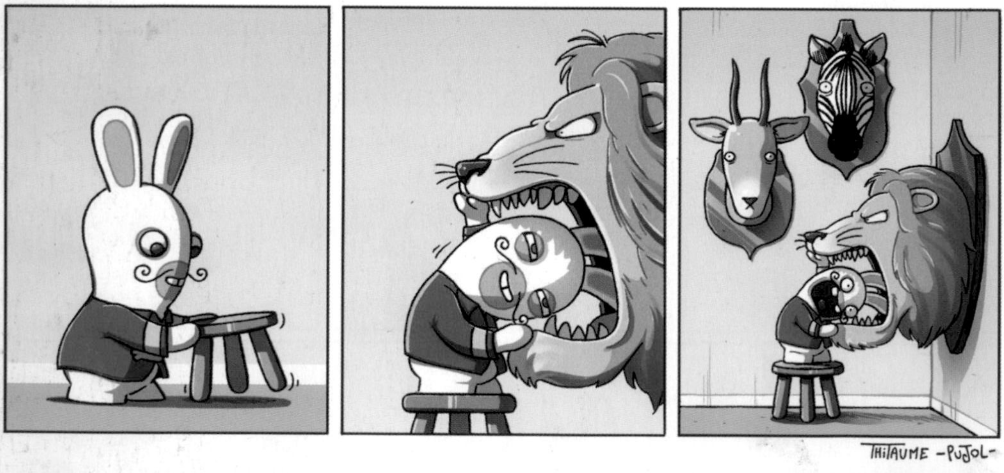
THITAUME -PUJOL-

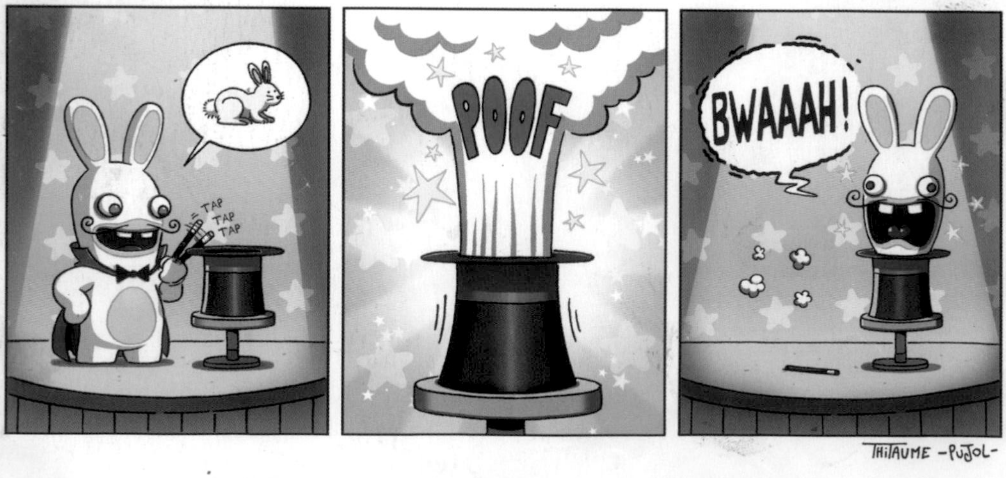
TAP
TAP
TAP
POOF
BWAAAH!
THITAUME -PUJOL-

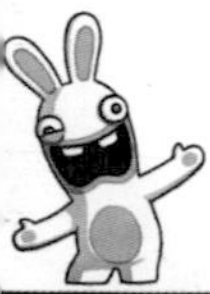

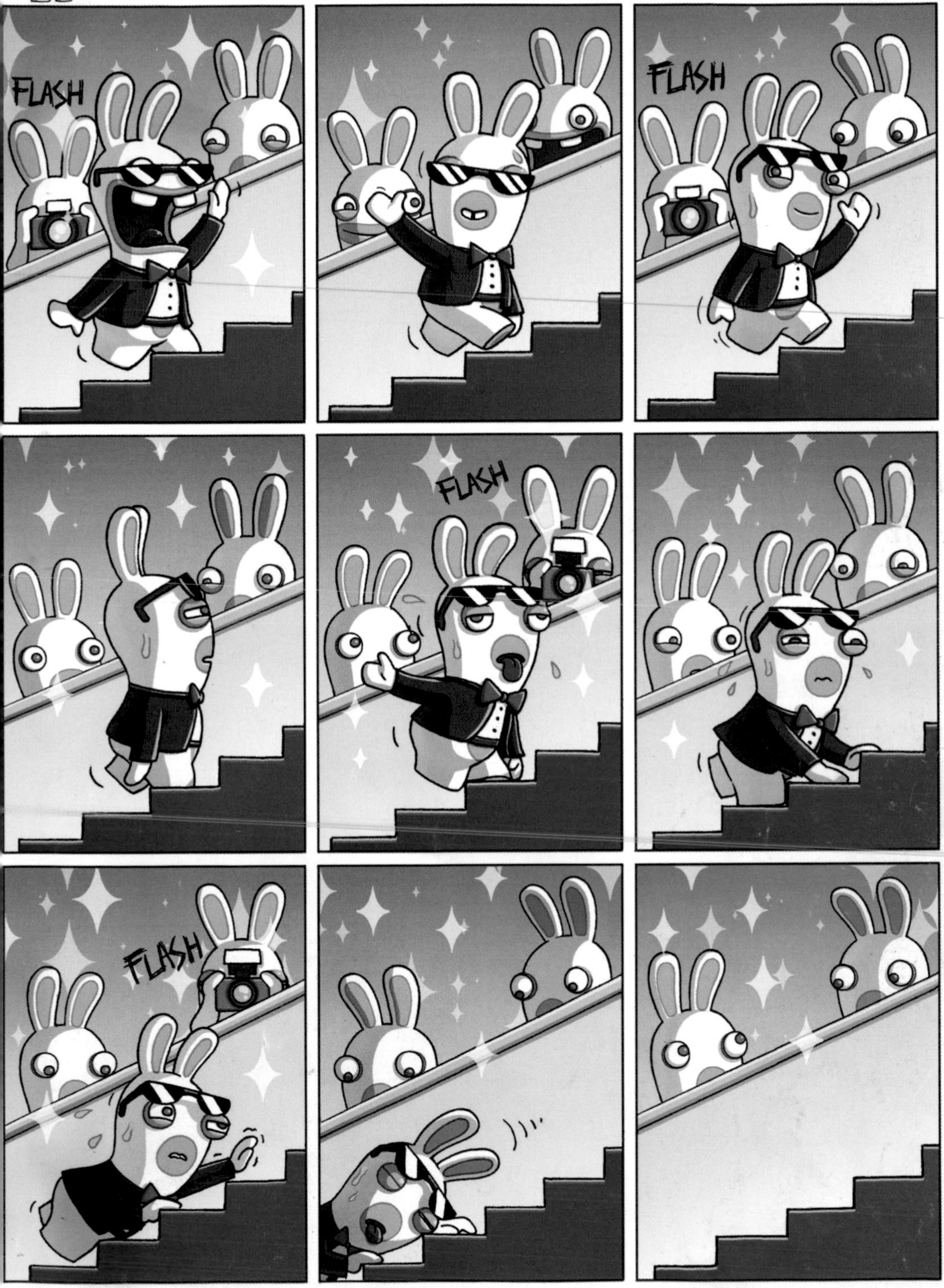
FLASH
FLASH
FLASH
FLASH

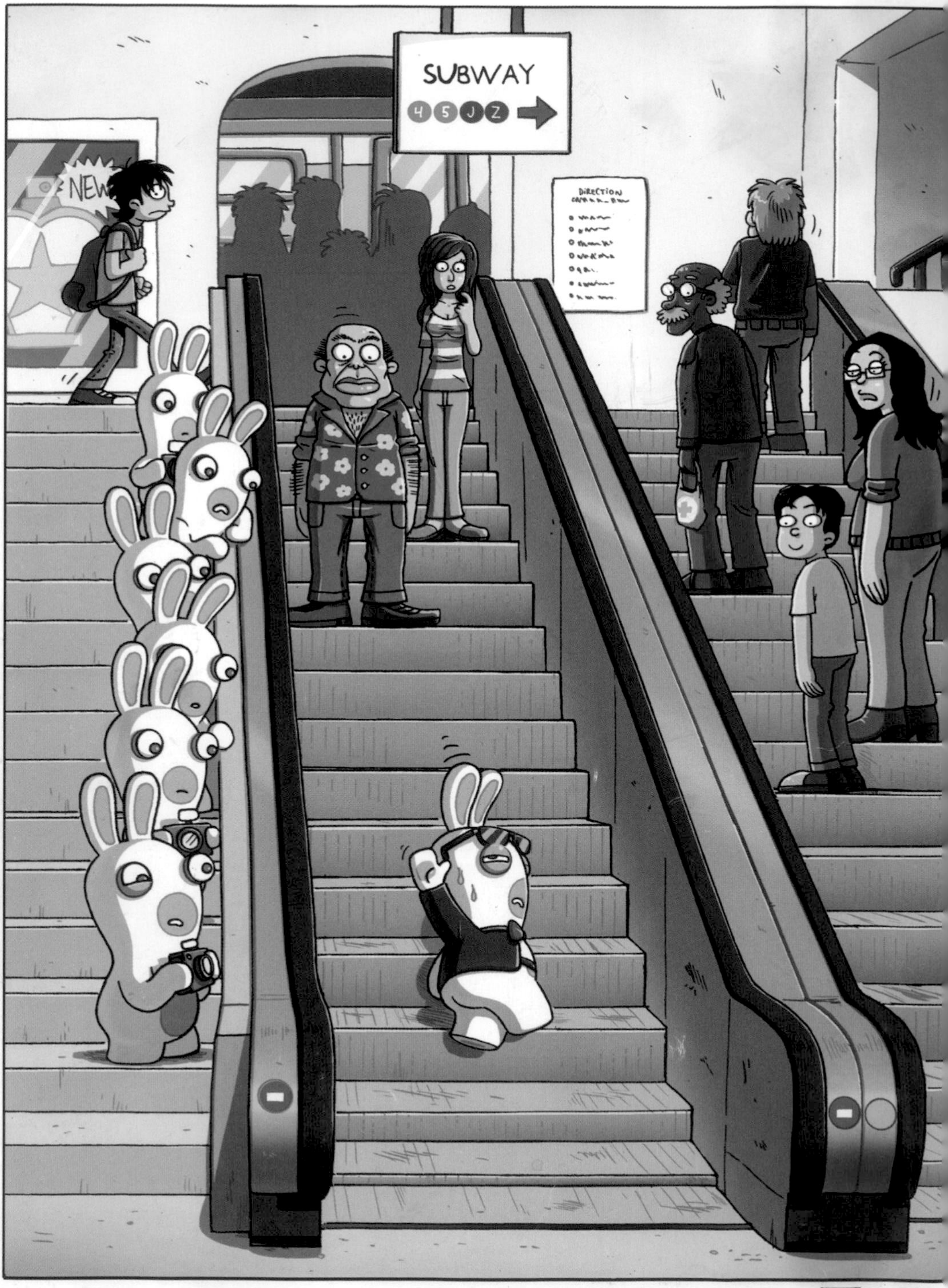
SUBWAY
4 5 J Z
NEW
DIRECTION
THITAUME -PUJOL-

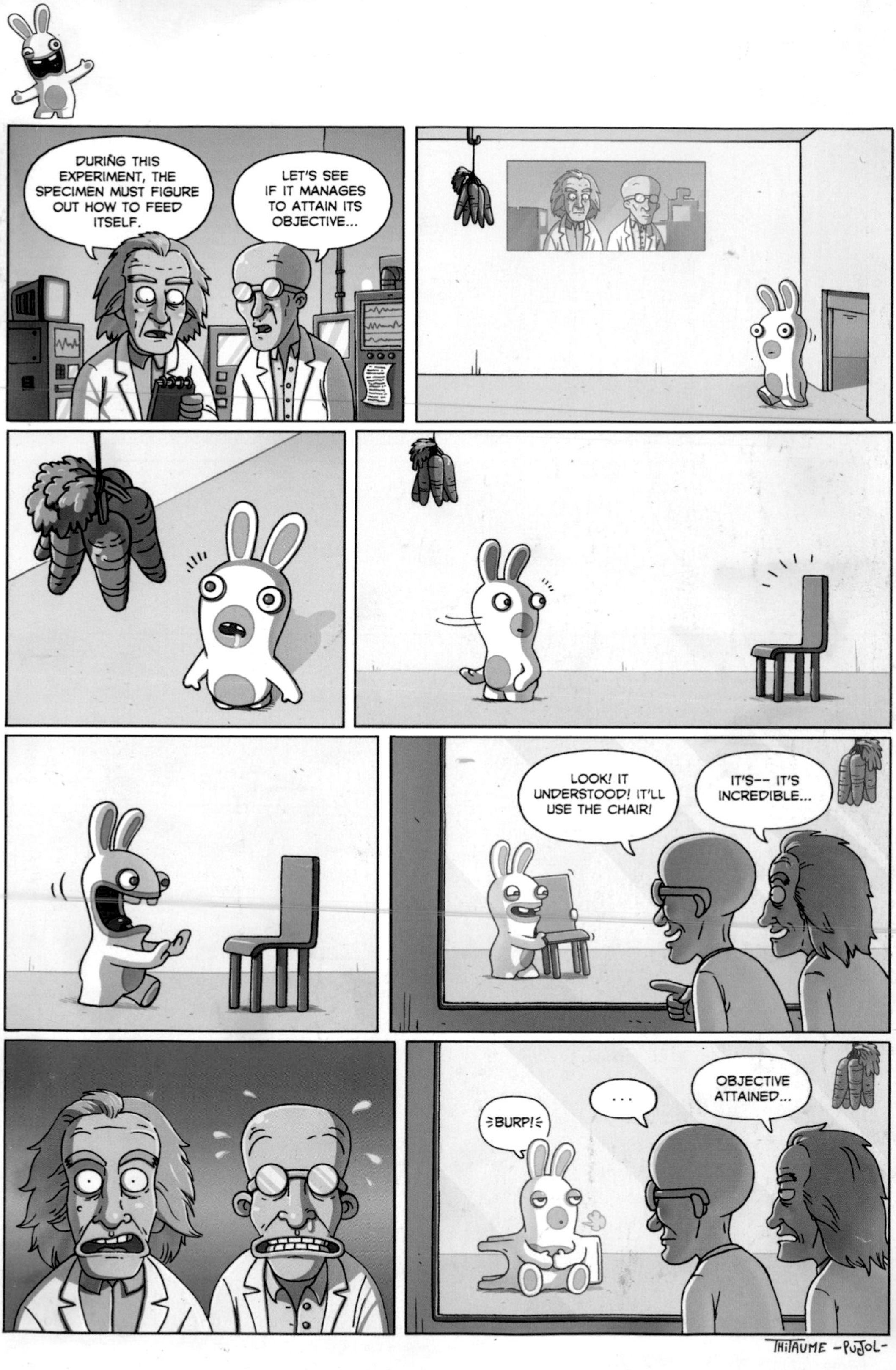
DURING THIS EXPERIMENT, THE SPECIMEN MUST FIGURE OUT HOW TO FEED ITSELF.
LET'S SEE IF IT MANAGES TO ATTAIN ITS OBJECTIVE...
LOOK! IT UNDERSTOOD! IT'LL USE THE CHAIR!
IT'S-- IT'S INCREDIBLE...
BURP!
...
OBJECTIVE ATTAINED...
THITAUME -PUJOL-

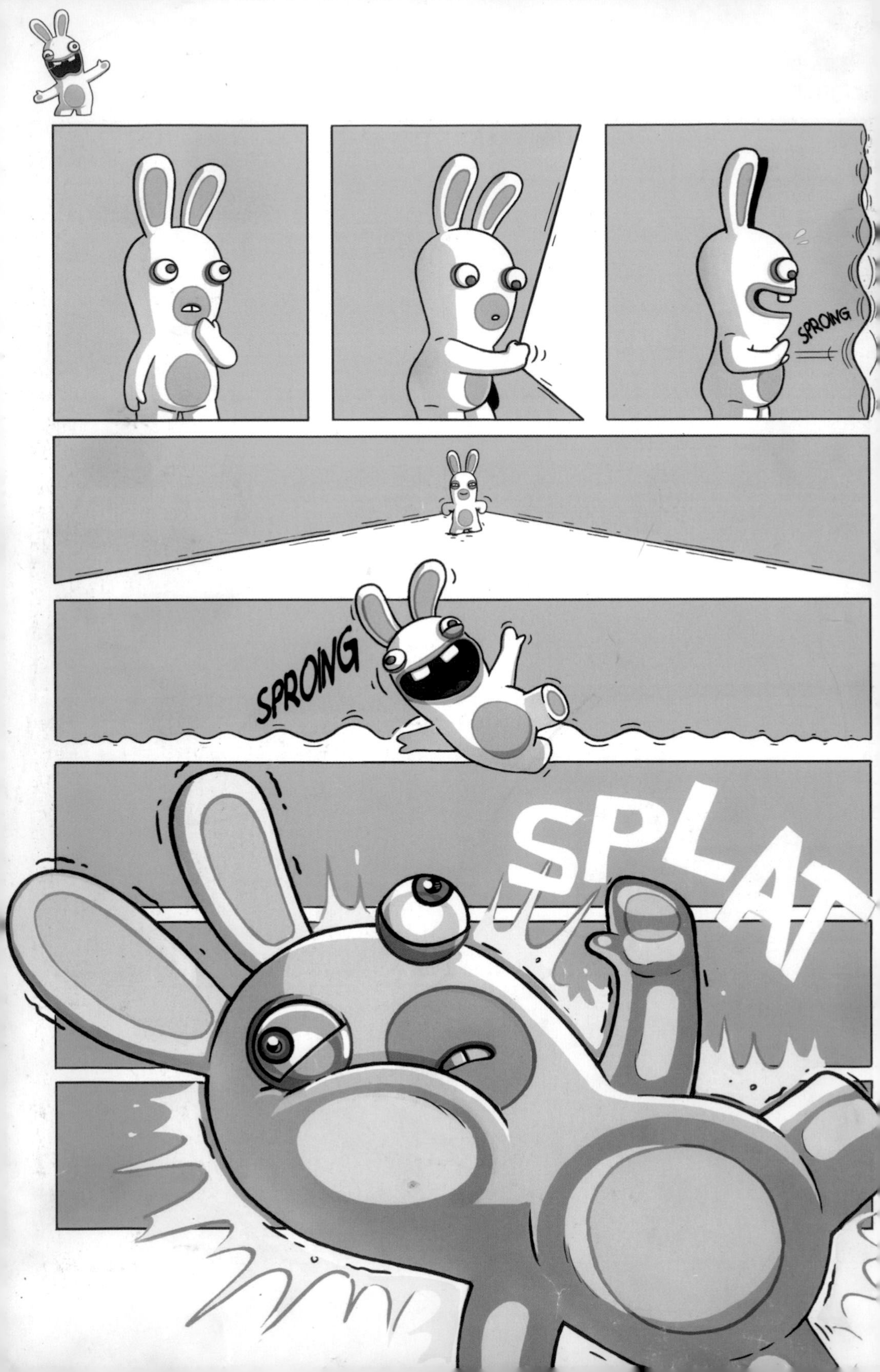
SPROING
SPROING
SPLAT

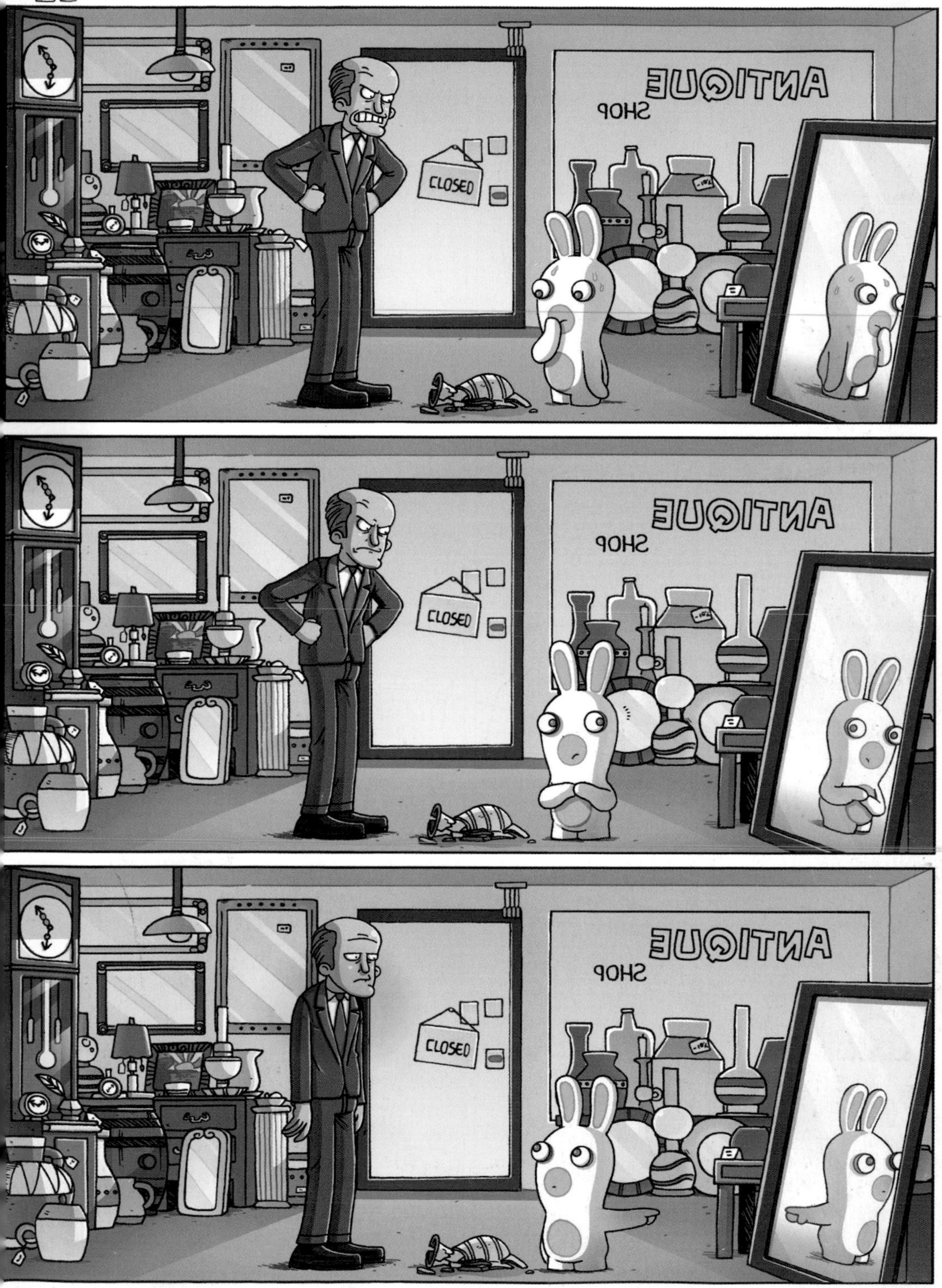
ANTIQUE
SHOP
CLOSED
ANTIQUE
SHOP
CLOSED
ANTIQUE
SHOP
CLOSED

THITAUME -PUJOL-

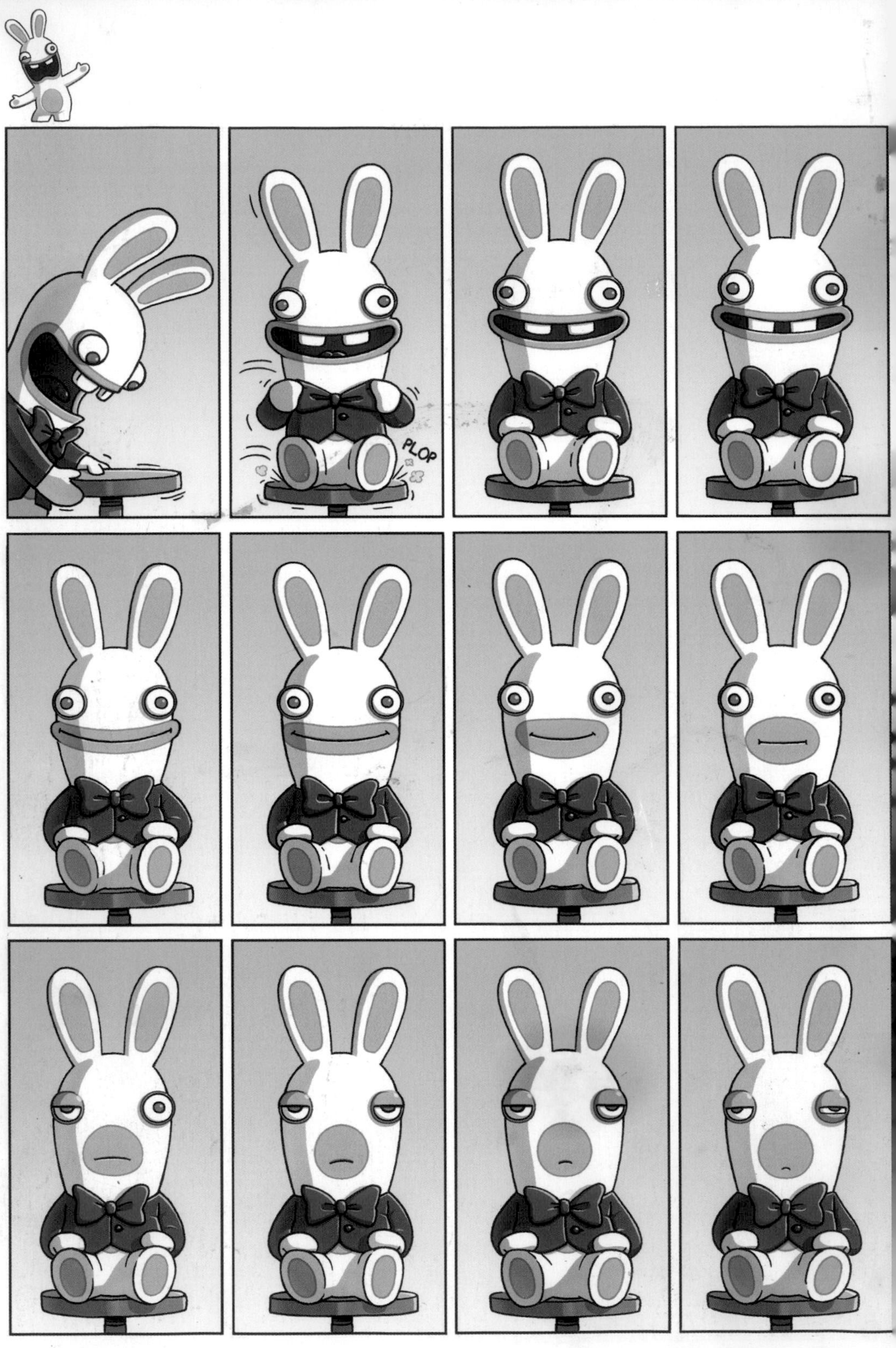
PLOP

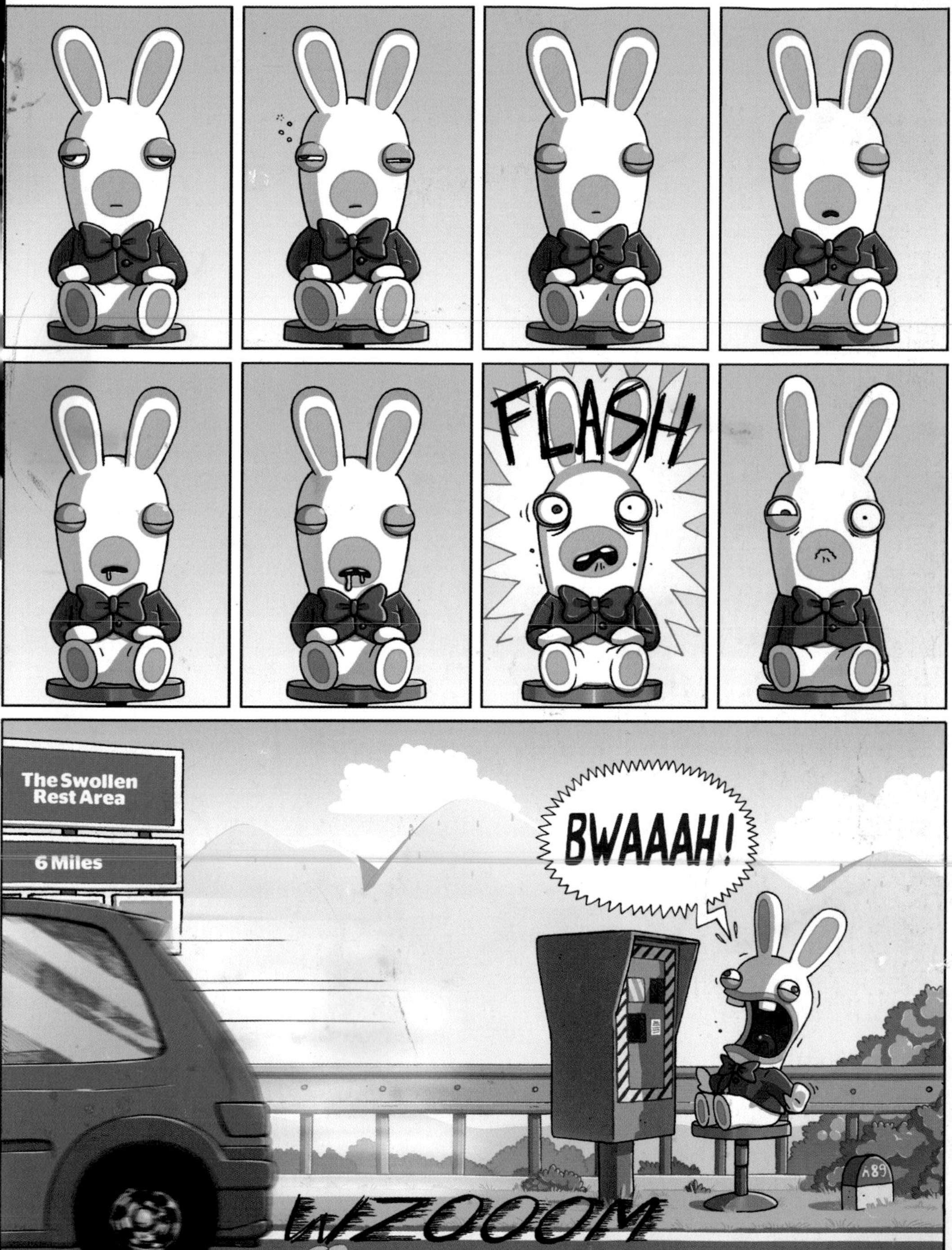
FLASH
The Swollen Rest Area
6 Miles
BWAAAH!
WZOOOM
THITAUME -PUJOL-

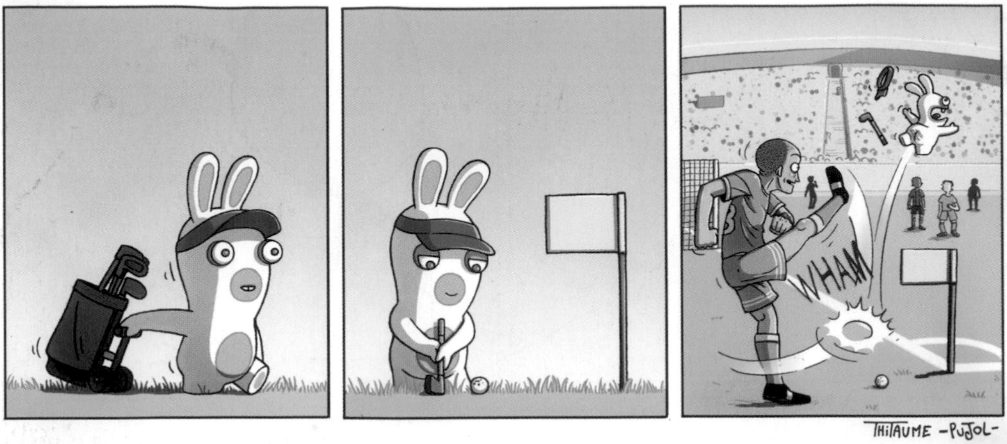
WHAM
THITAUME -PUJOL-

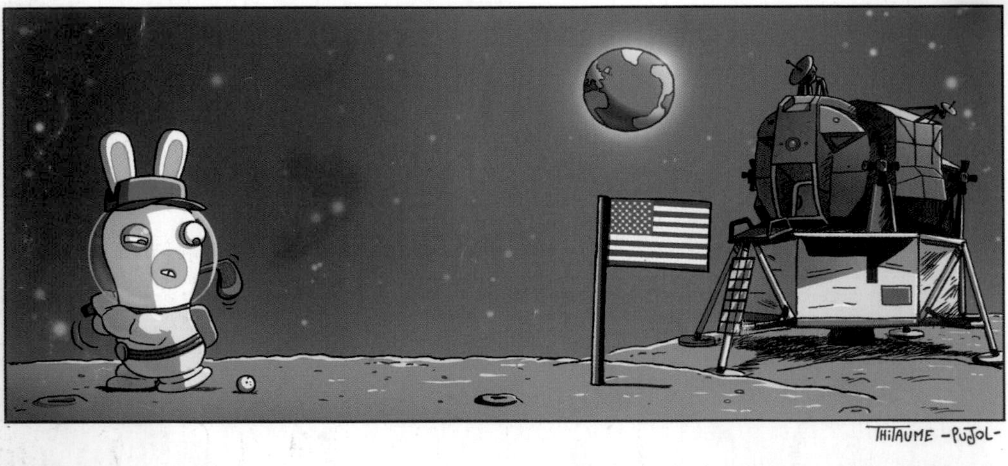
THITAUME -PUJOL-

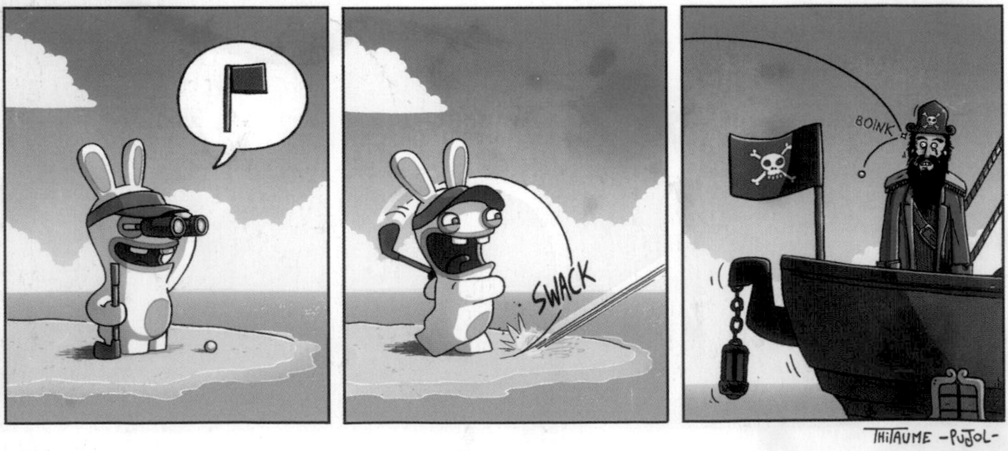
SWACK
BOINK
THITAUME -PUJOL-

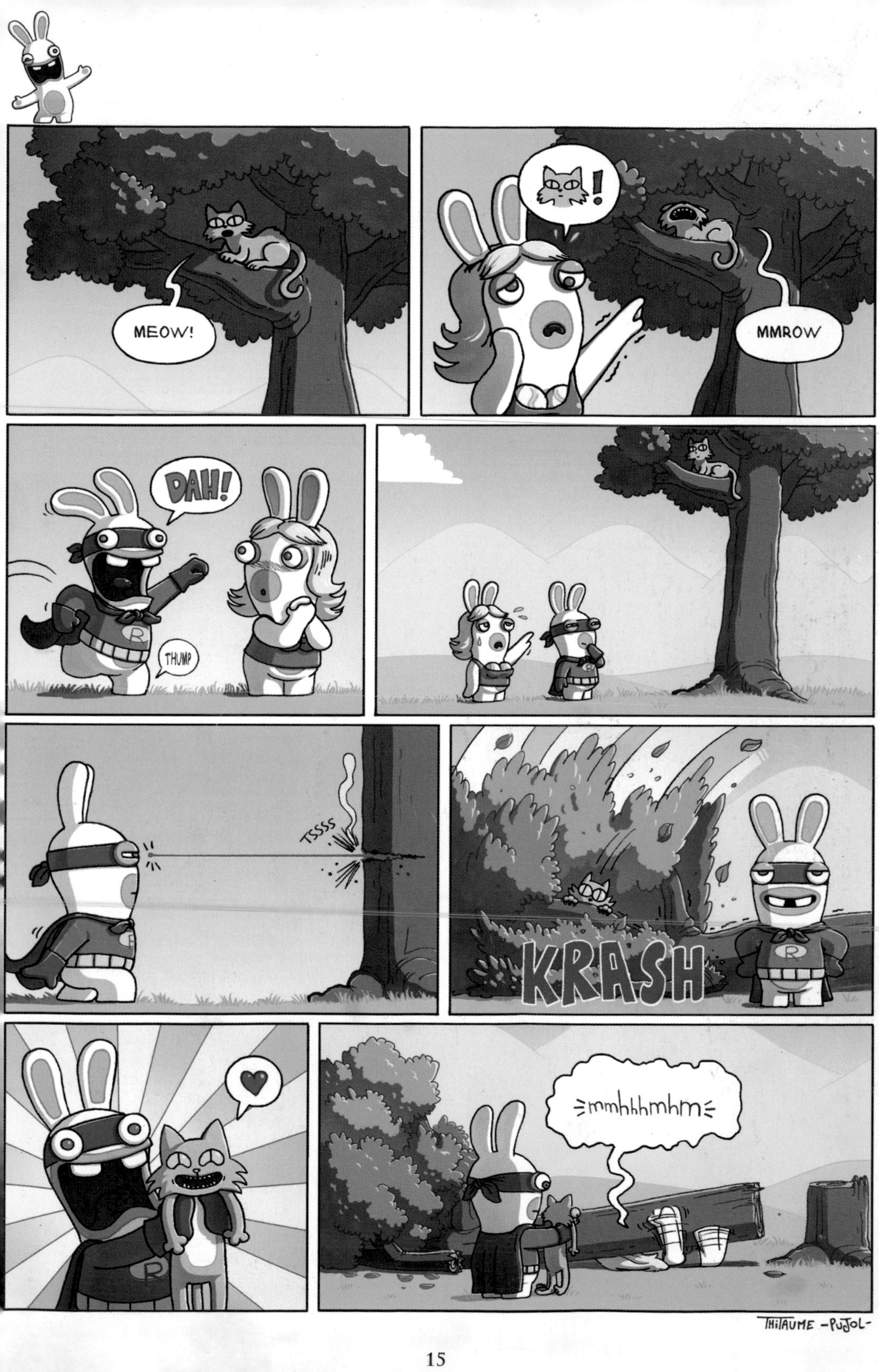
MEOW!
!
MMROW
DAH!
THUMP
TSSSS
KRASH
mmhhhmhm

THITAUME -PUJOL-

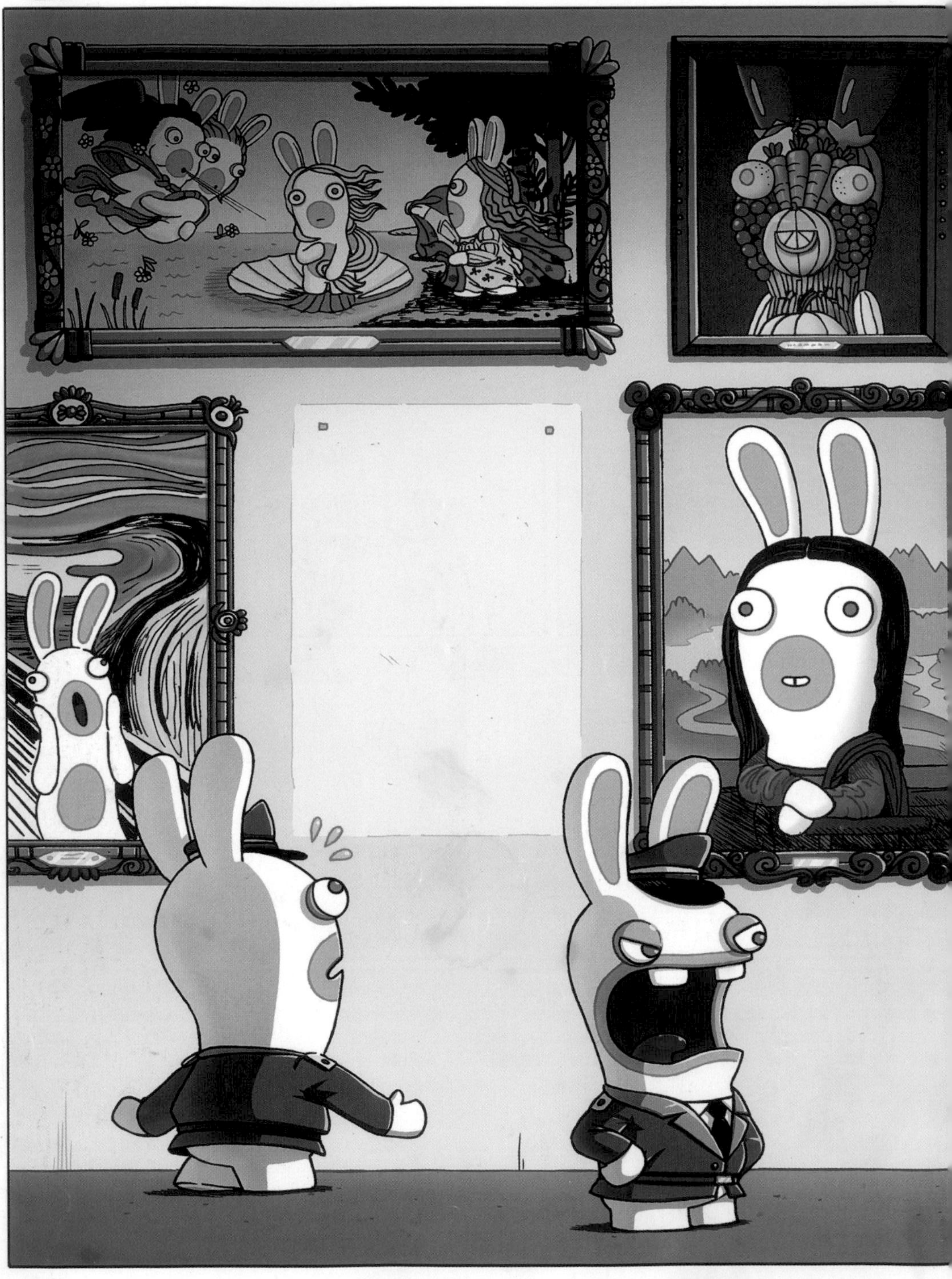

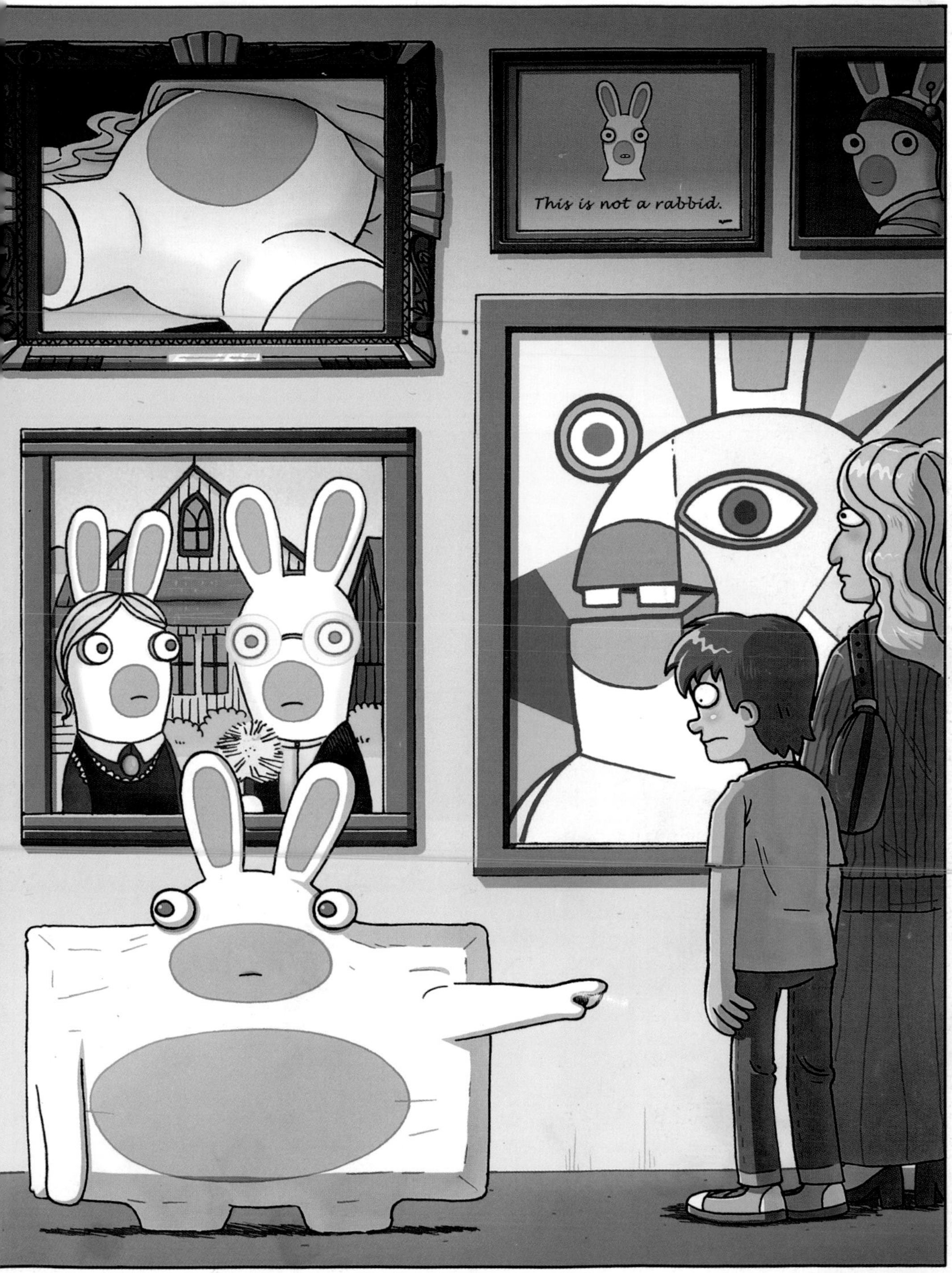
This is not a rabbid.

THITAUME -PUJOL-

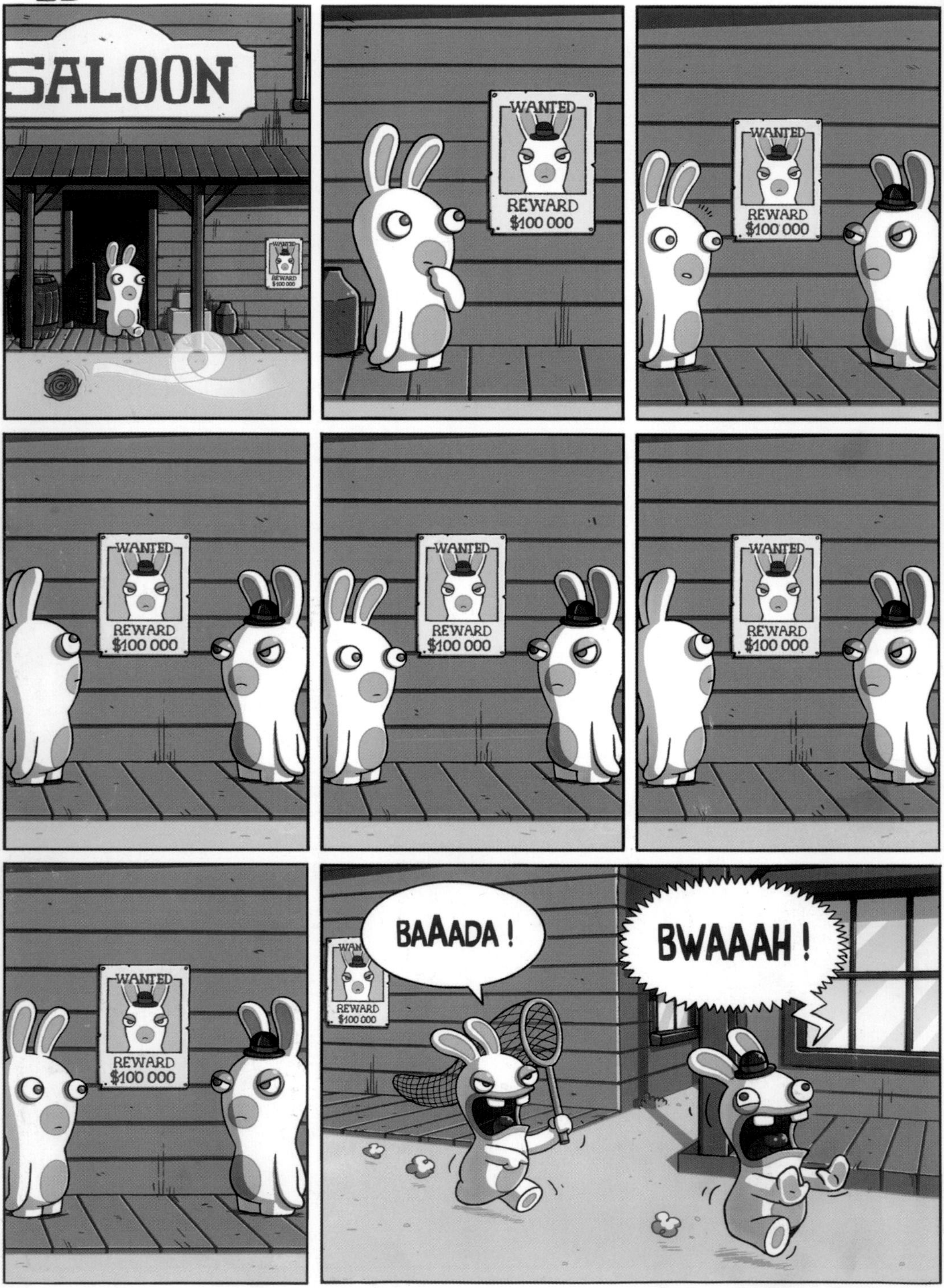
SALOON
WANTED
REWARD
$100 000
WANTED
REWARD
$100 000
WANTED
REWARD
$100 000
WANTED
REWARD
$100 000
WANTED
REWARD
$100 000
WANTED
REWARD
$100 000
BAAADA !
BWAAAH !

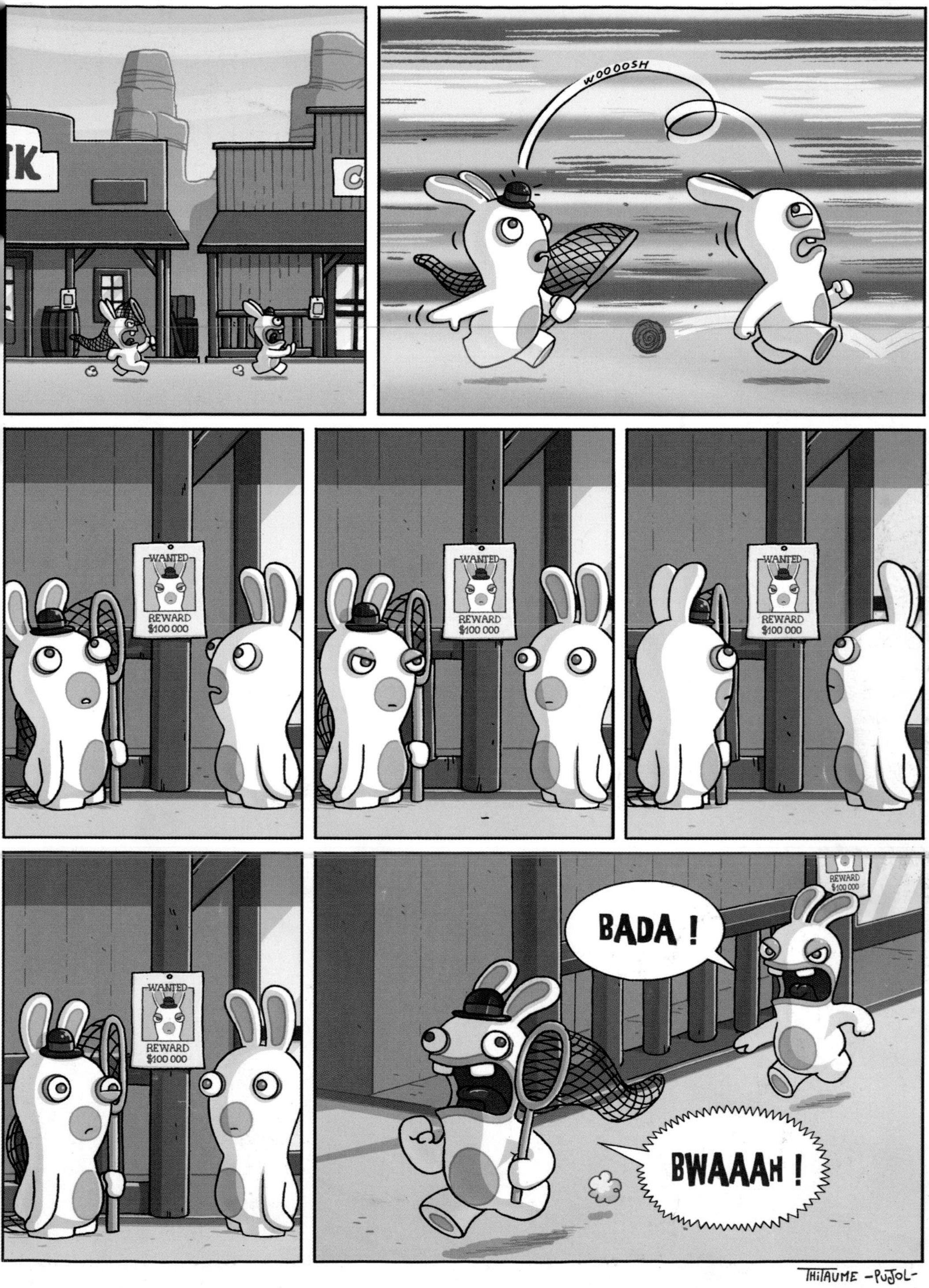
WOOOOSH
WANTED
REWARD
$100 000
BADA !
BWAAAH !
THILAUME -PUJOL-

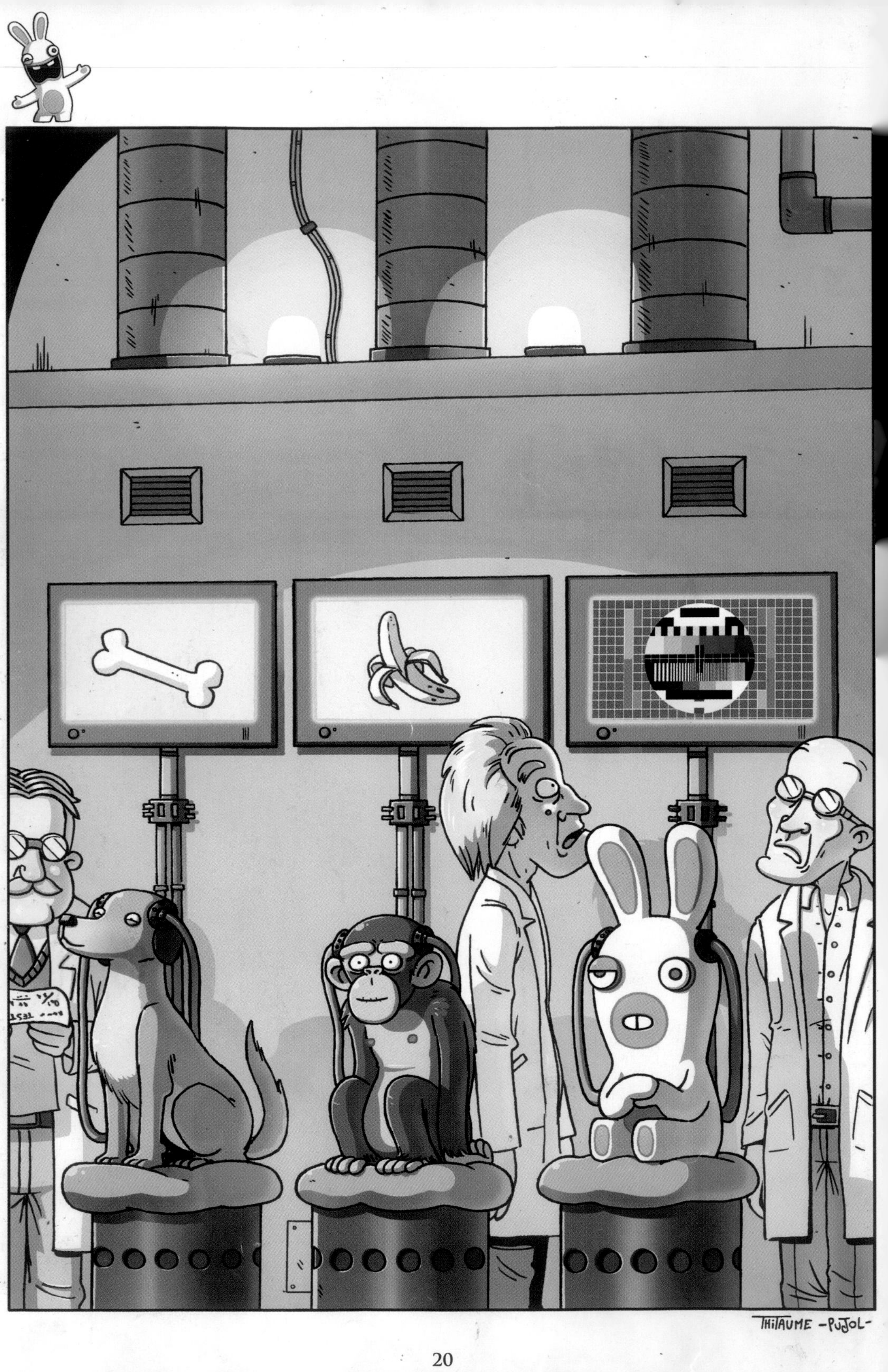

THITAUME -PUJOL-

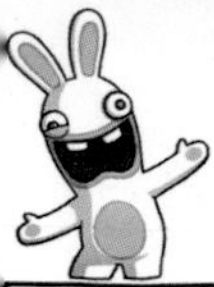

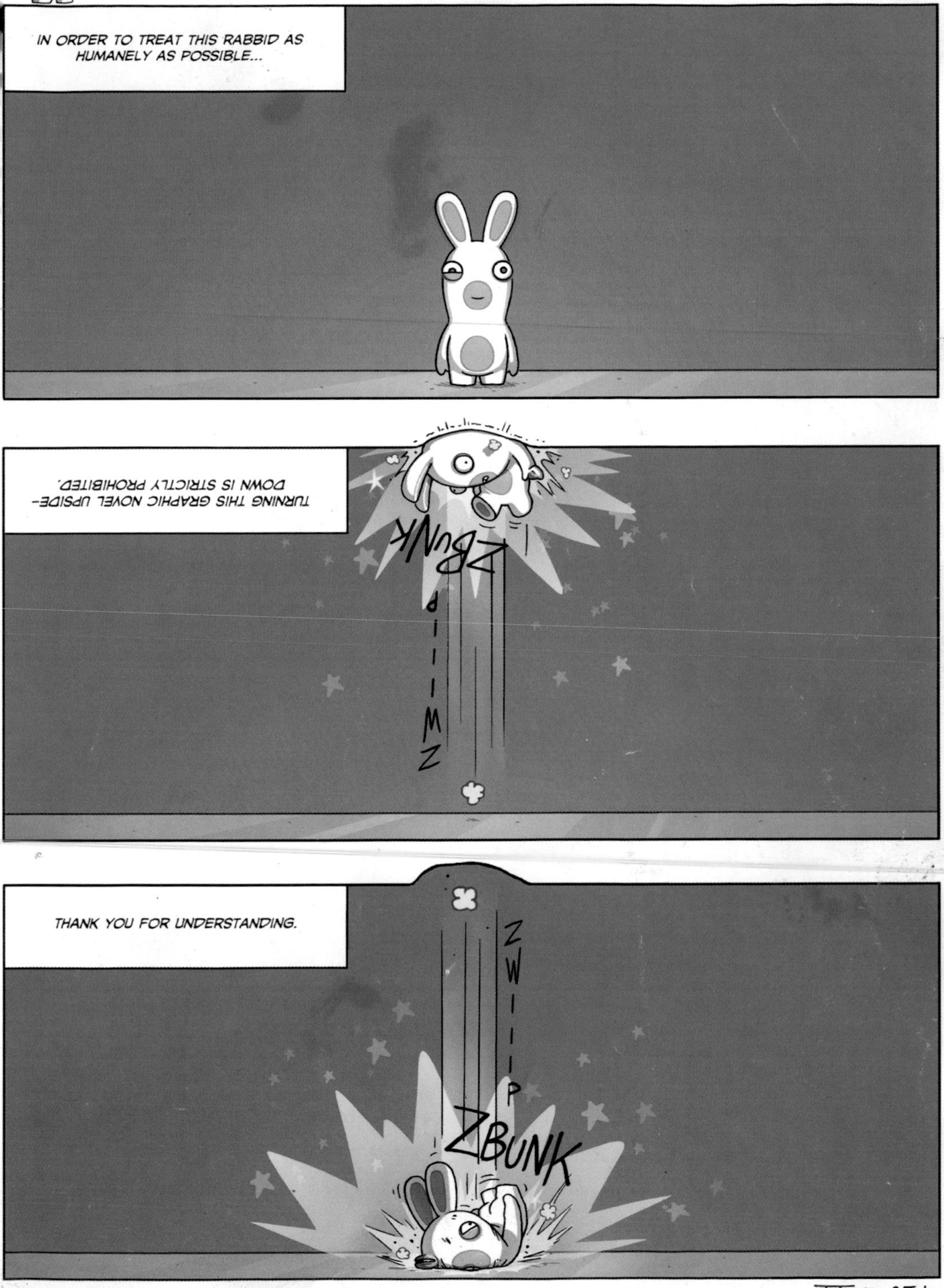

IN ORDER TO TREAT THIS RABBID AS HUMANELY AS POSSIBLE...
TURNING THIS GRAPHIC NOVEL UPSIDE-DOWN IS STRICTLY PROHIBITED.
ZBUNK
ZWIIIP
THANK YOU FOR UNDERSTANDING.
ZWIIIP
ZBUNK


THITAUME -PUJOL-

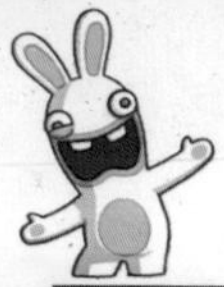

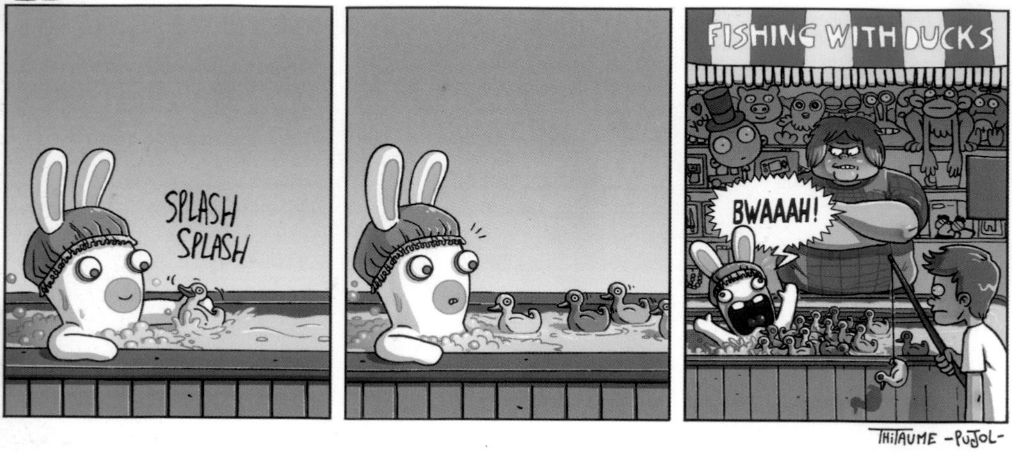
SPLASH
SPLASH
FISHING WITH DUCKS
BWAAAH!
THITAUME -PUJOL-

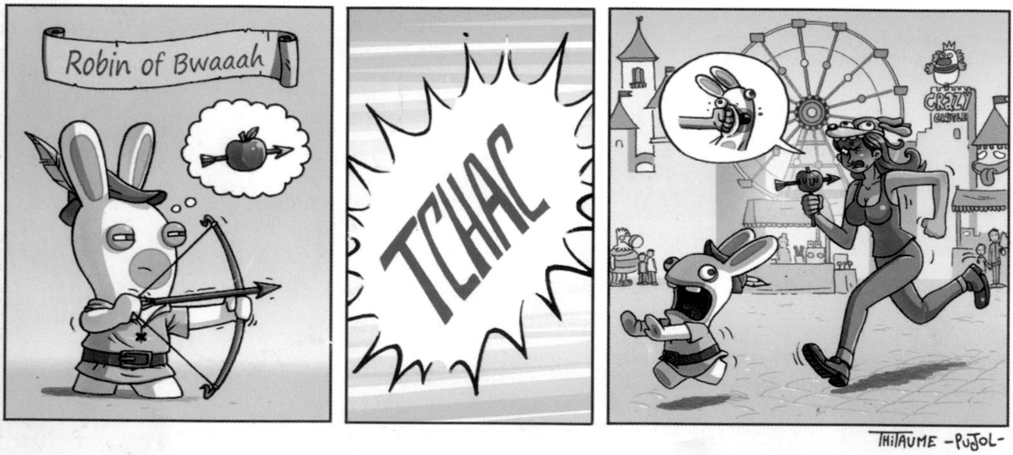
Robin of Bwaaah
TCHAC
CRAZY
THITAUME -PUJOL-

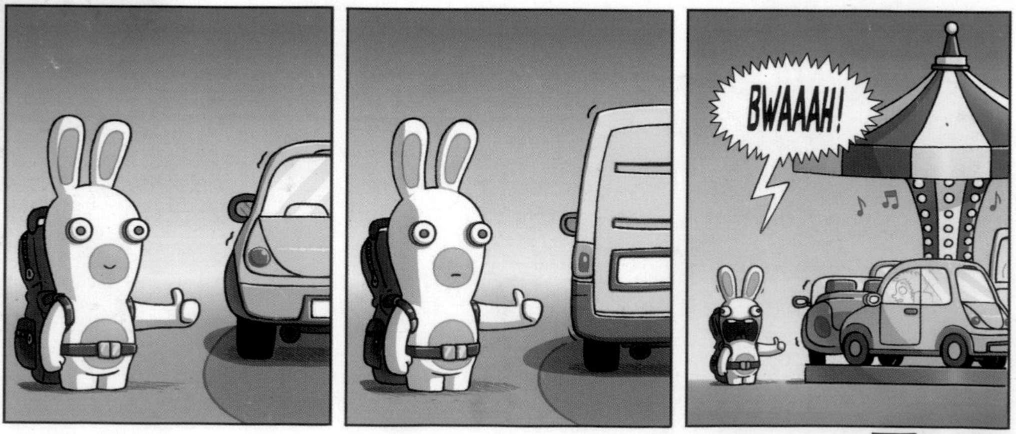
BWAAAH!
THITAUME -PUJOL-

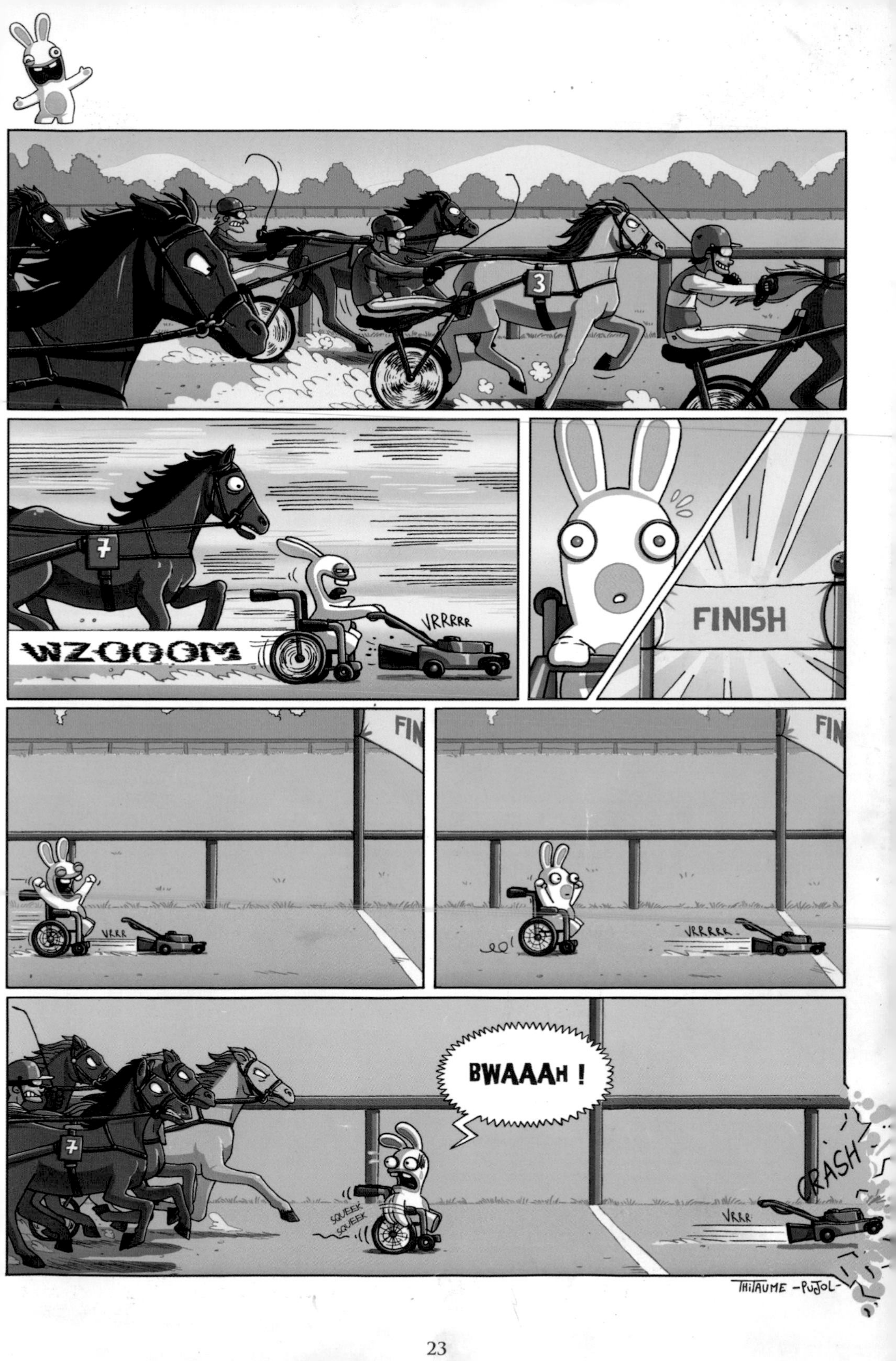
3
7
WZOOOM
VRRRRR
FINISH
FIN
VRRR
FIN
VRRRRR
7
BWAAAH !
SQUEEK SQUEEK
VRRR
CRASH
THITAUME -PUJOL-

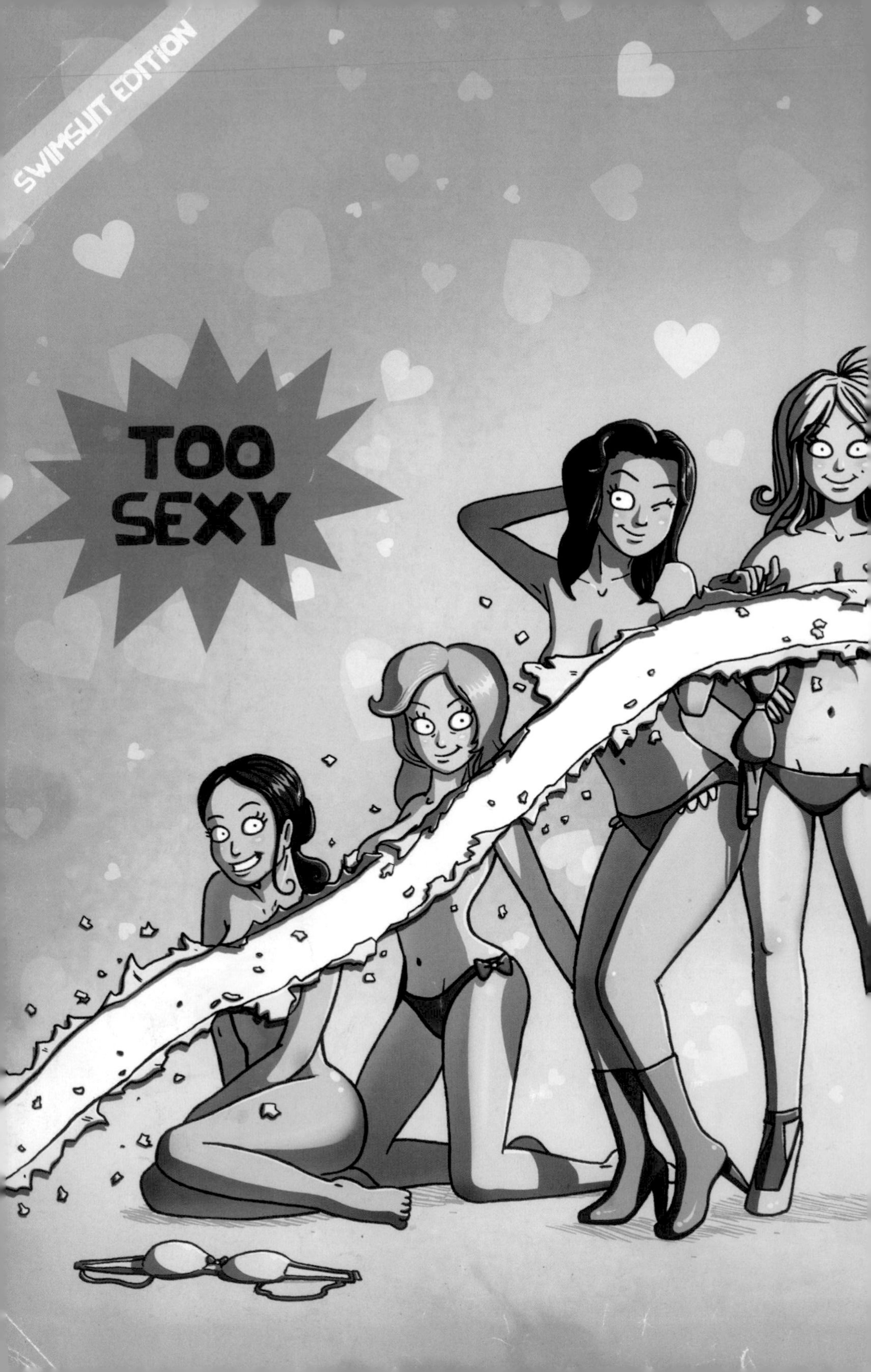
SWIMSUIT EDITION
TOO SEXY

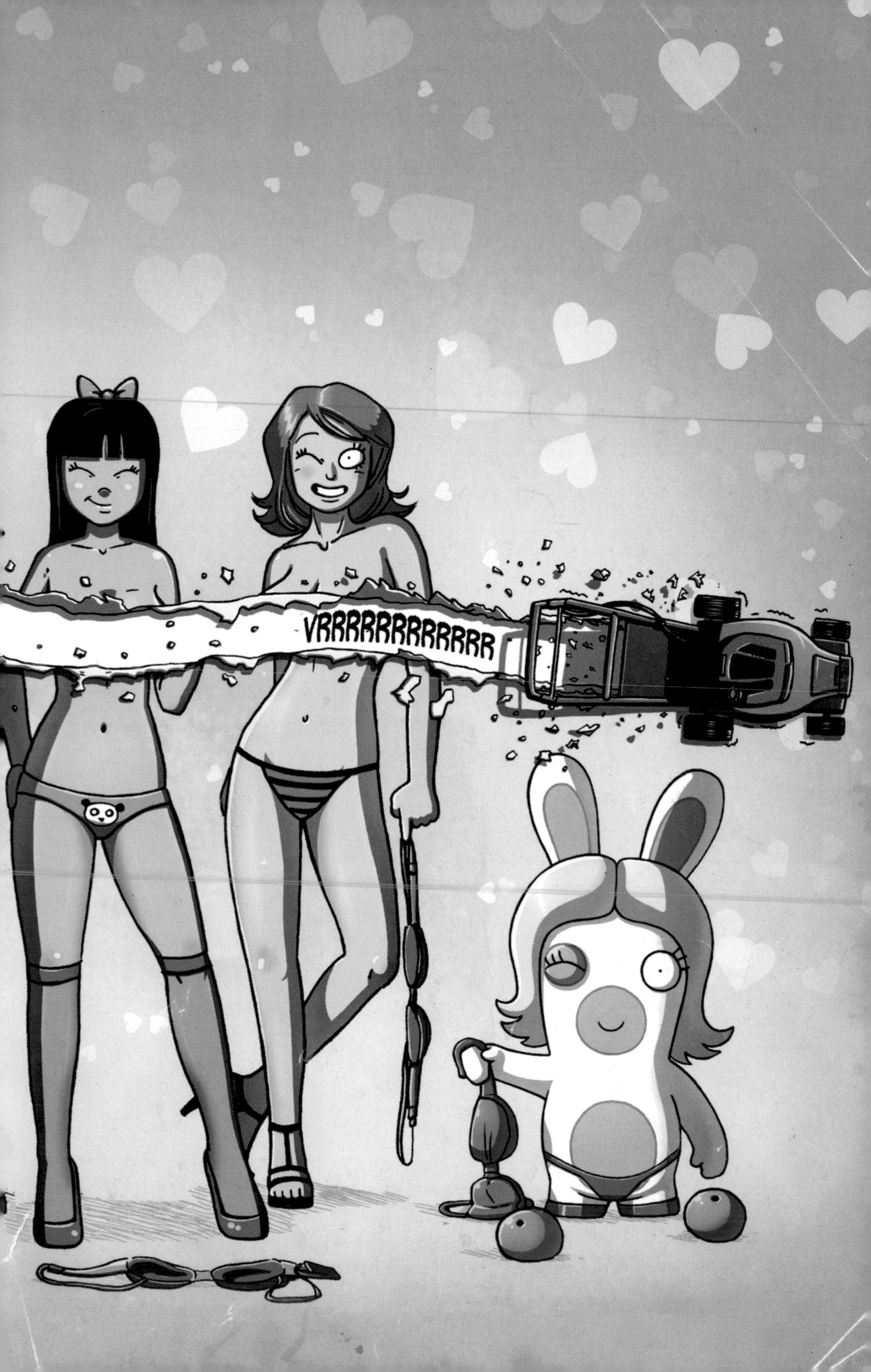
VRRRRRRRRRRRR

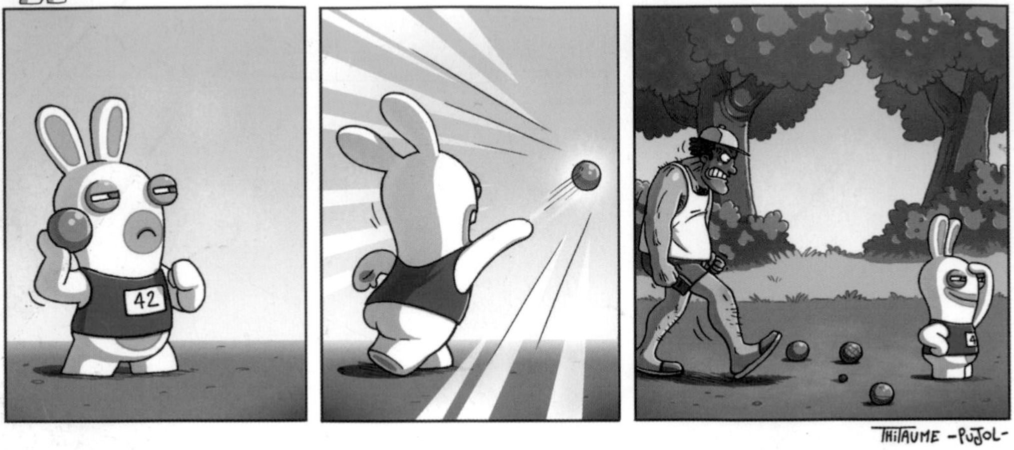
42
THITAUME -PUJOL-

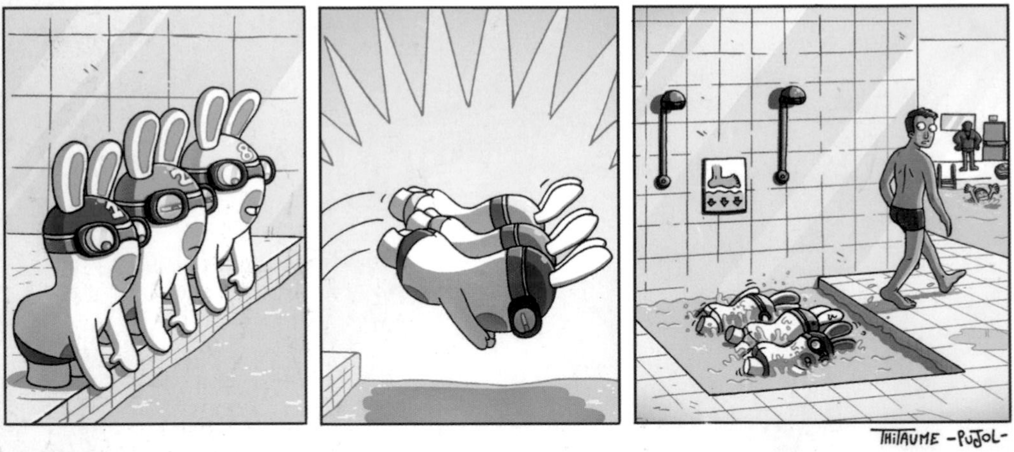
THITAUME -PUJOL-

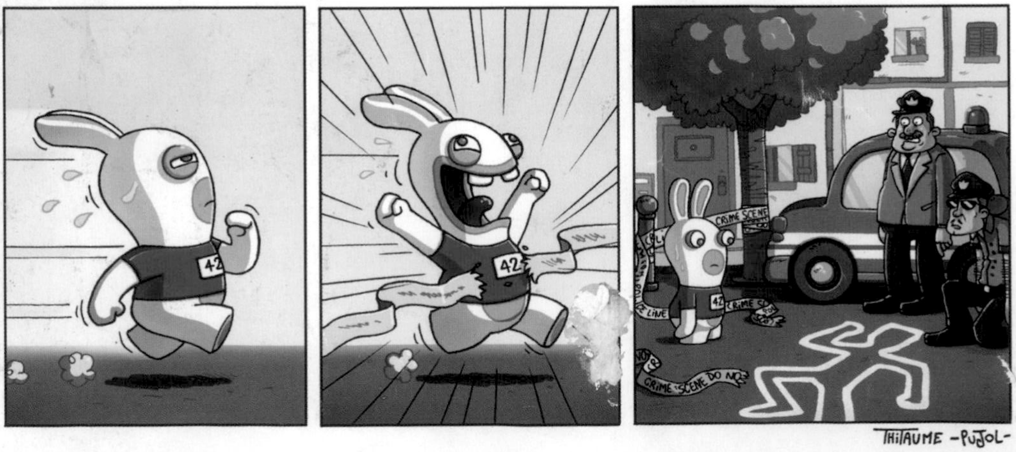
42
42
CRIME SCENE
CRIME SCENE DO NOT
THITAUME -PUJOL-

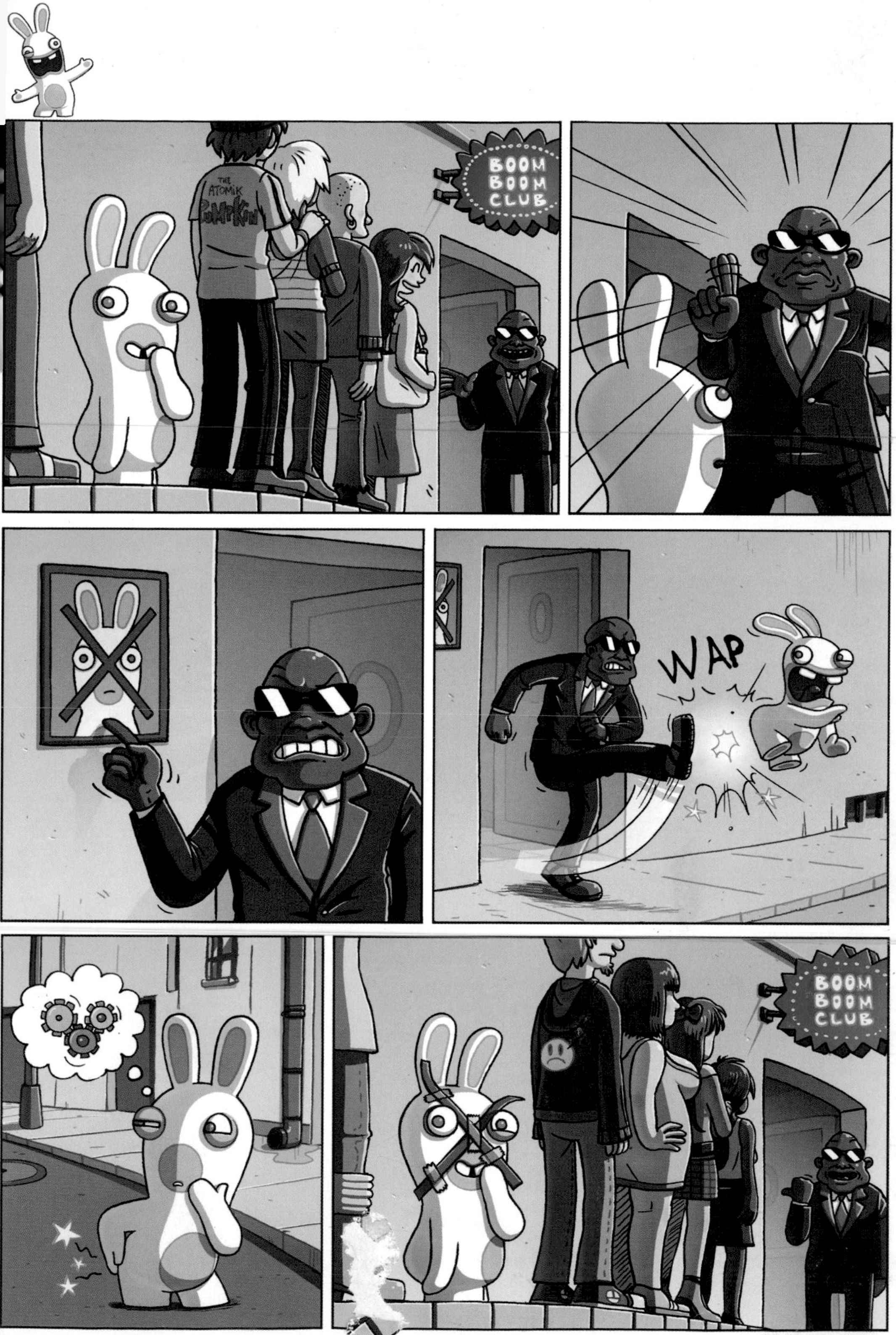
BOOM BOOM CLUB
THE ATOMIK PUMPKIN
WAP
BOOM BOOM CLUB

THITAUME -PUJOL-

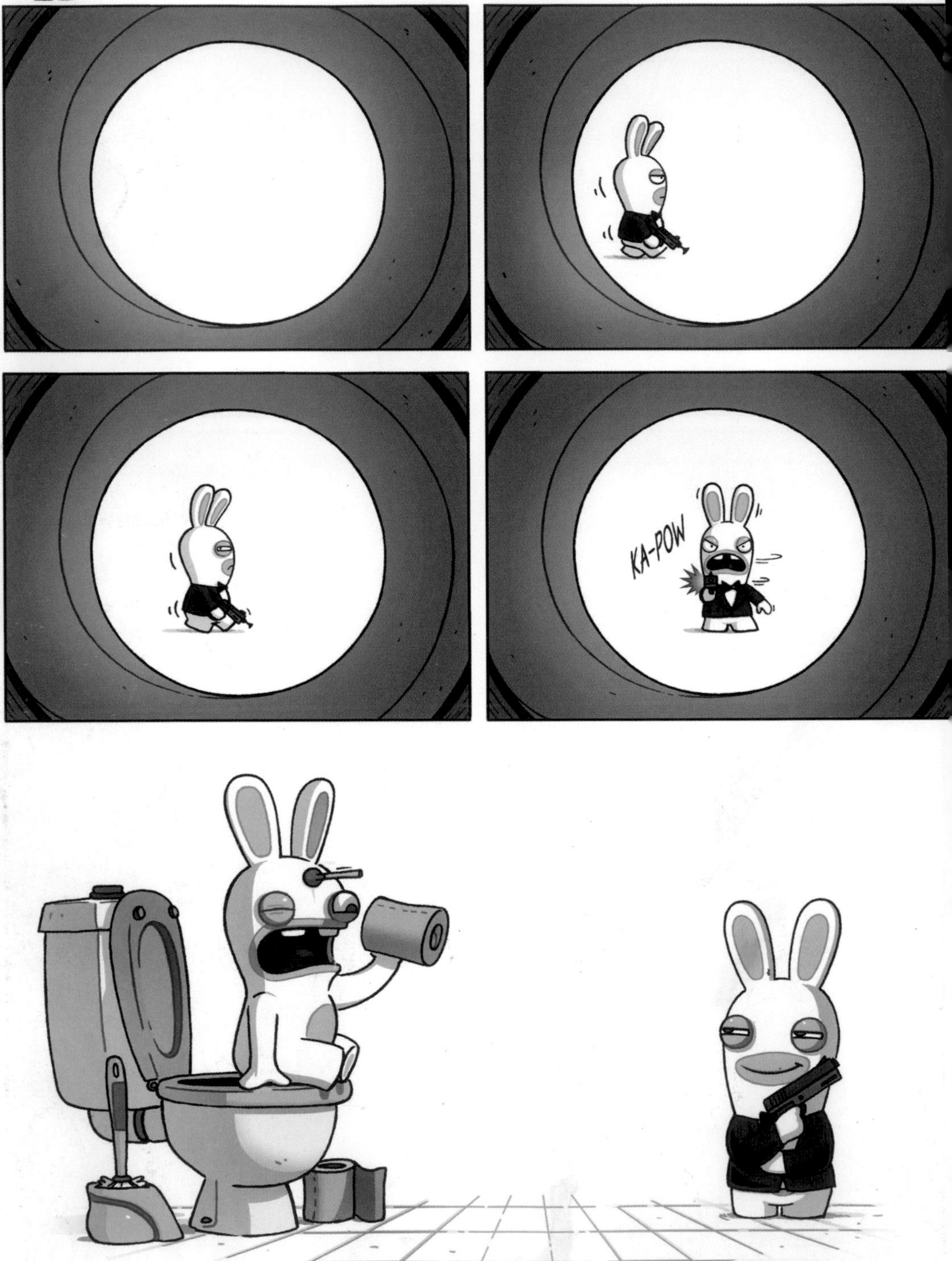
KA-POW
THITAUME -PUJOL-

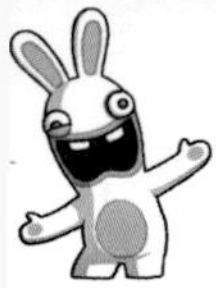

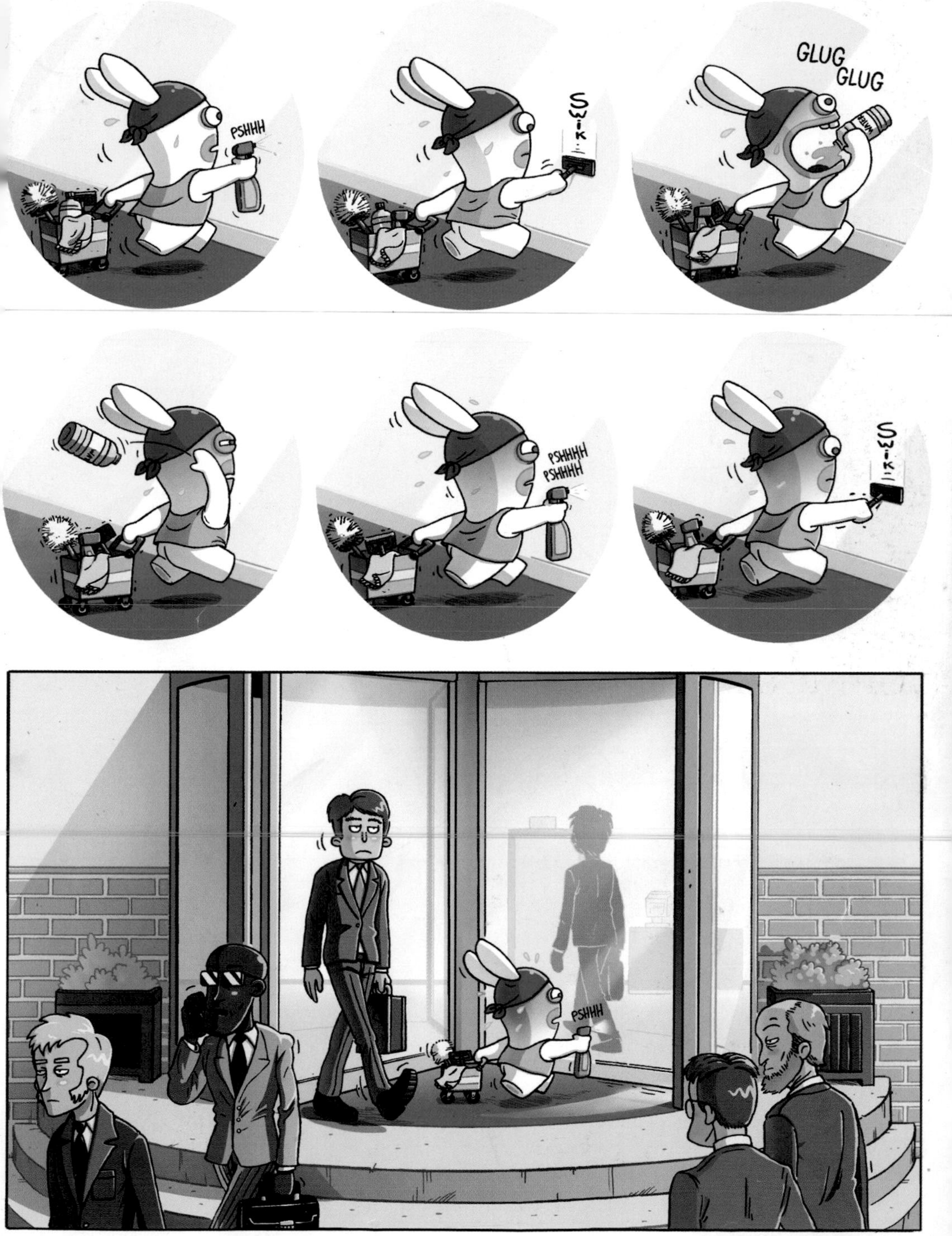
PSHHH
SWIK
GLUG
GLUG
PSHHHH
PSHHHH
SWIK
PSHHH
THILAUME -PUJOL-

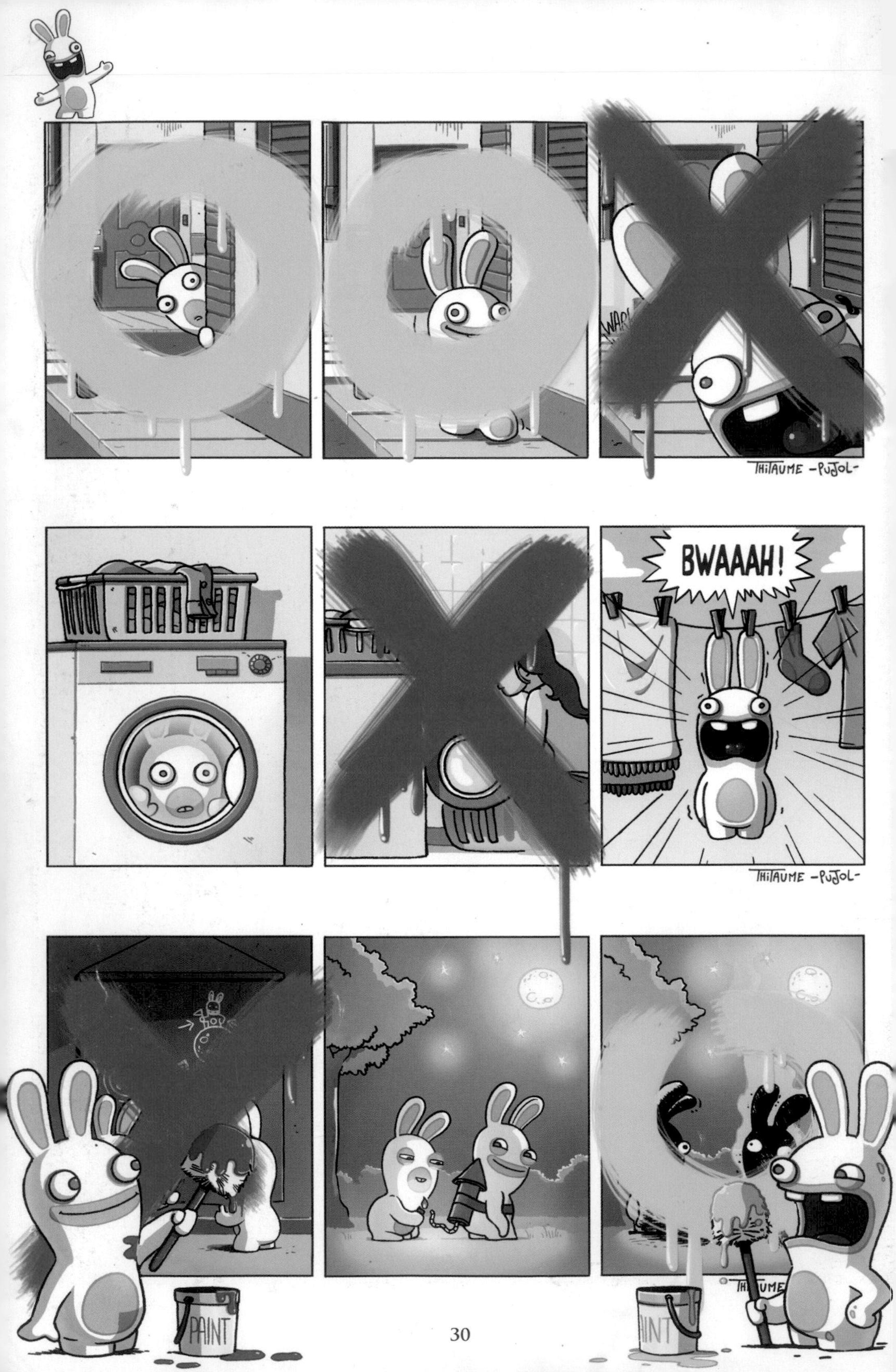
THITAUME -PUJOL-
BWAAAH!
THITAUME -PUJOL-
PAINT
PAINT

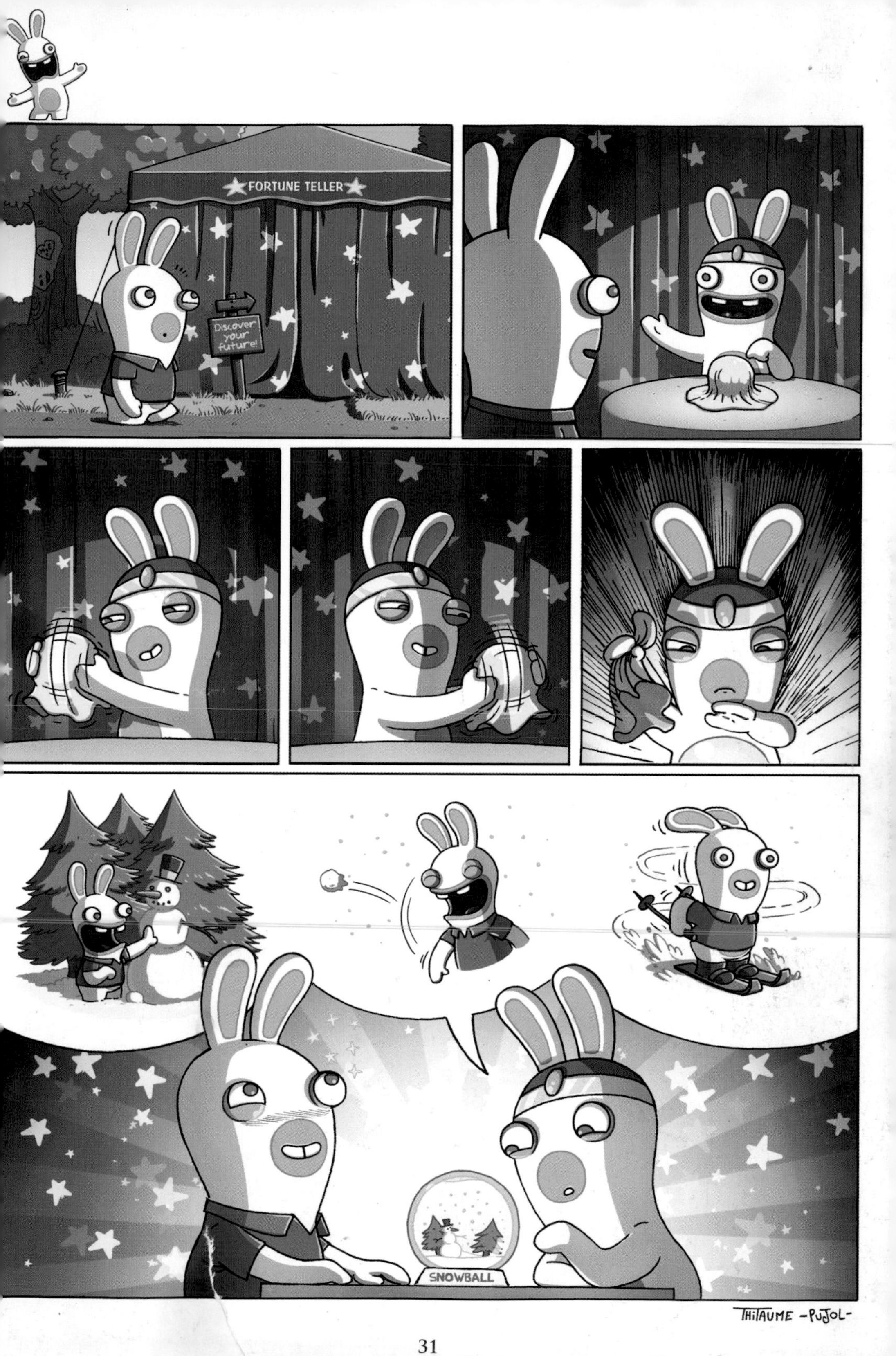
FORTUNE TELLER
Discover your future!
SNOWBALL
THITAUME -PUJOL-

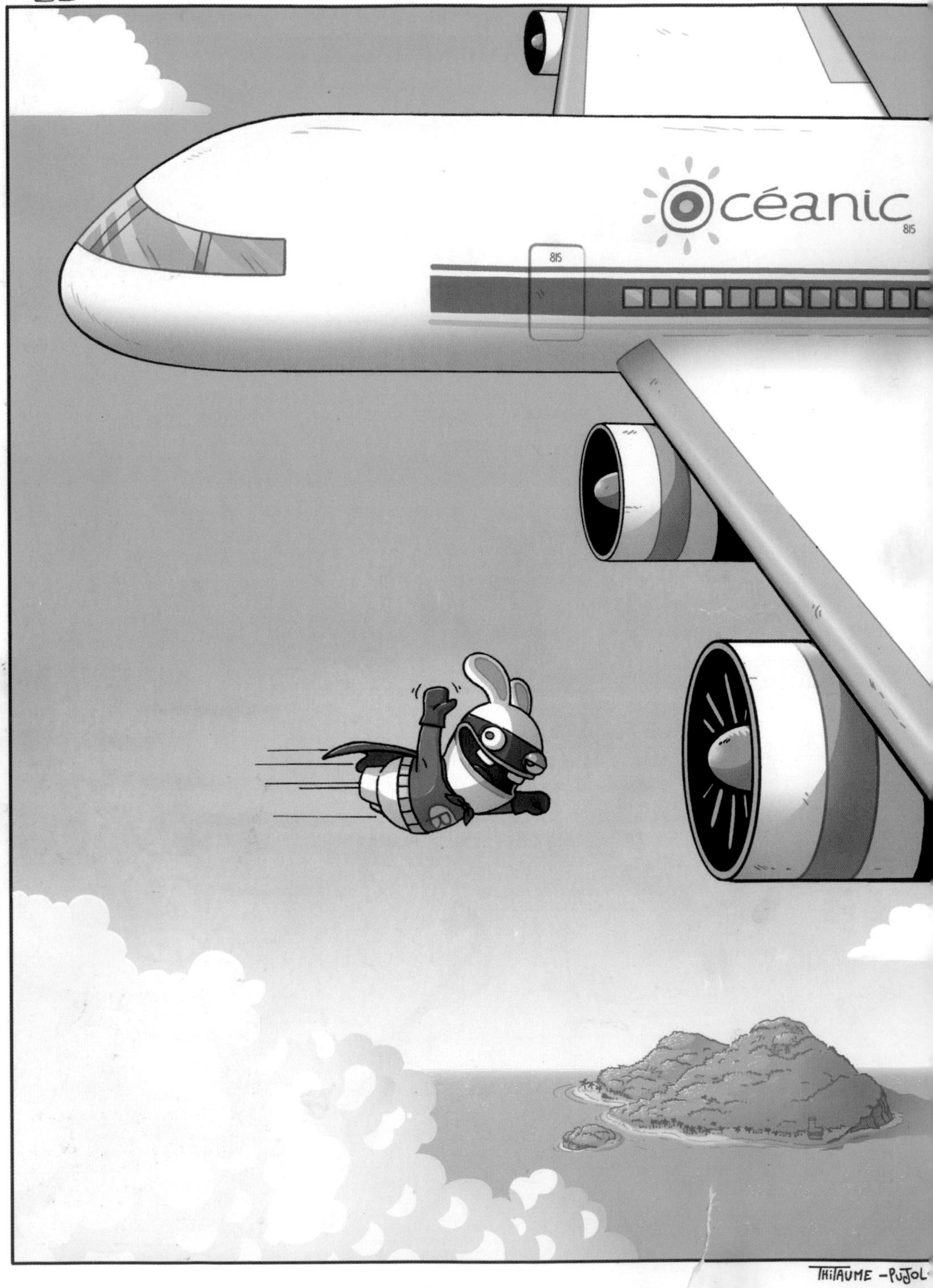
Océanic
815
815
THITAUME - PUJOL

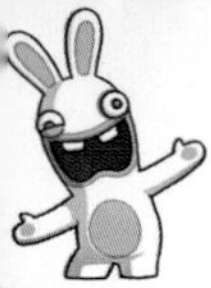

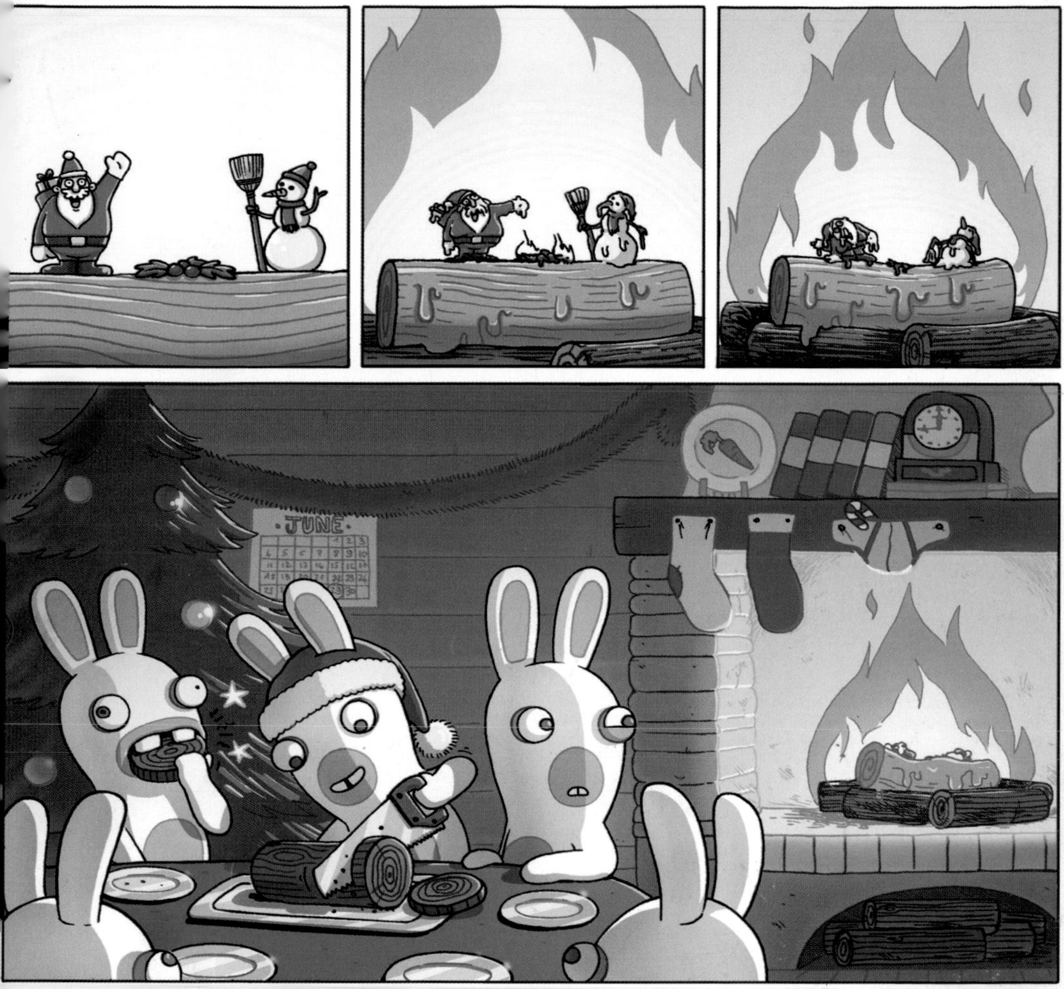
JUNE

THILAUME -PUJOL-

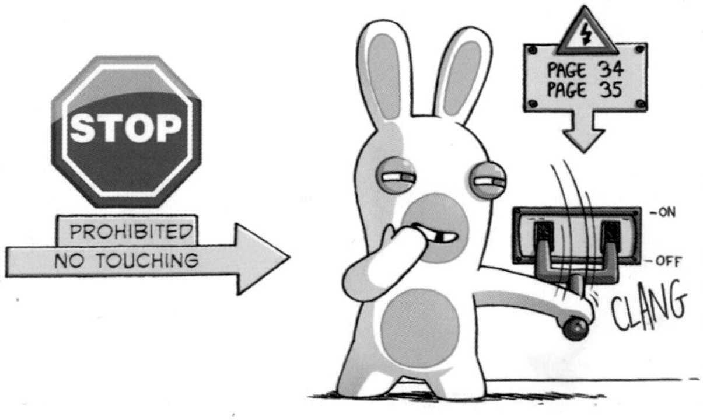
STOP
PROHIBITED
NO TOUCHING
PAGE 34
PAGE 35
-ON
-OFF
CLANG

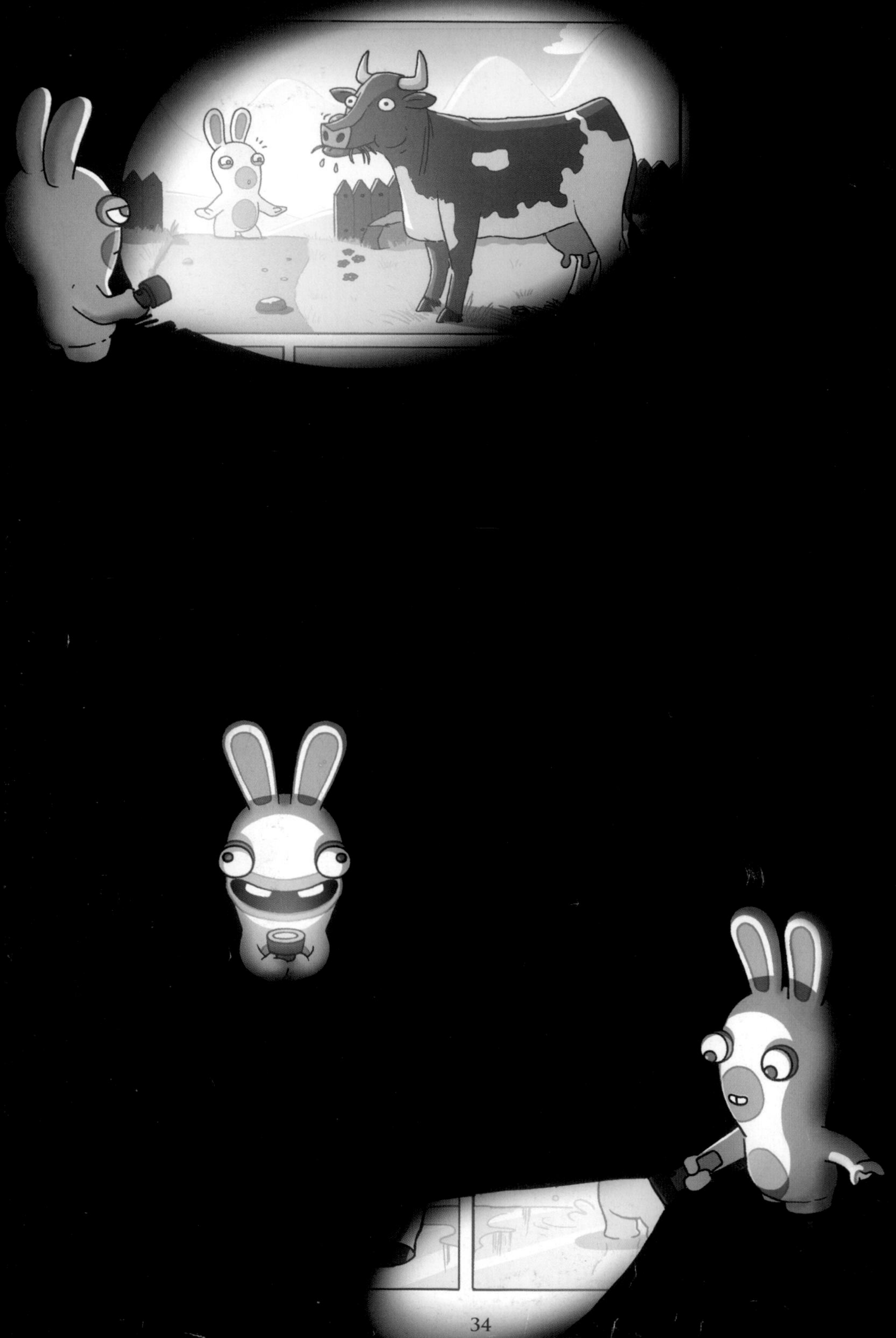

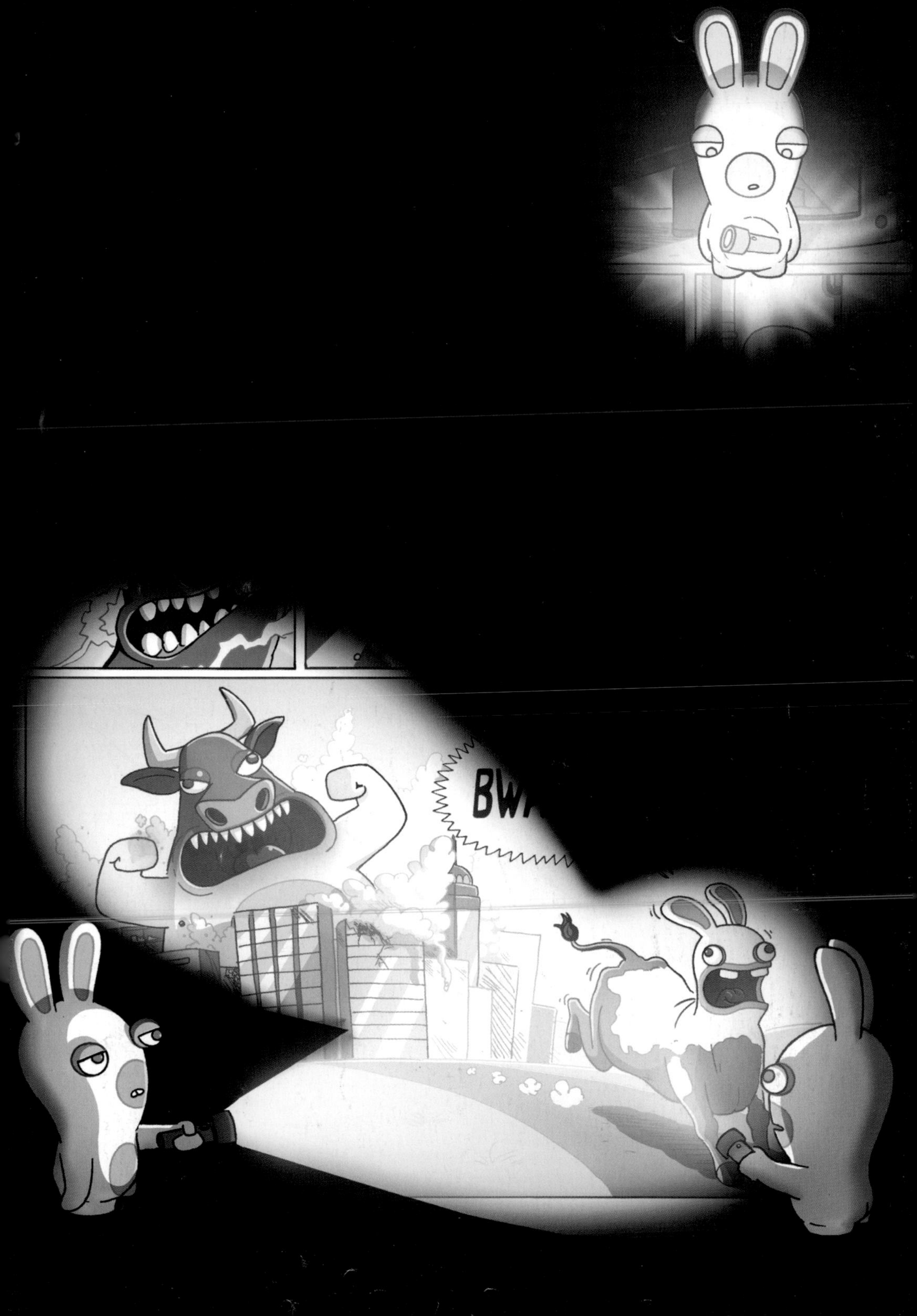

# WHERE'S BWAAALDO?

ThiTAUME -PUJOL-

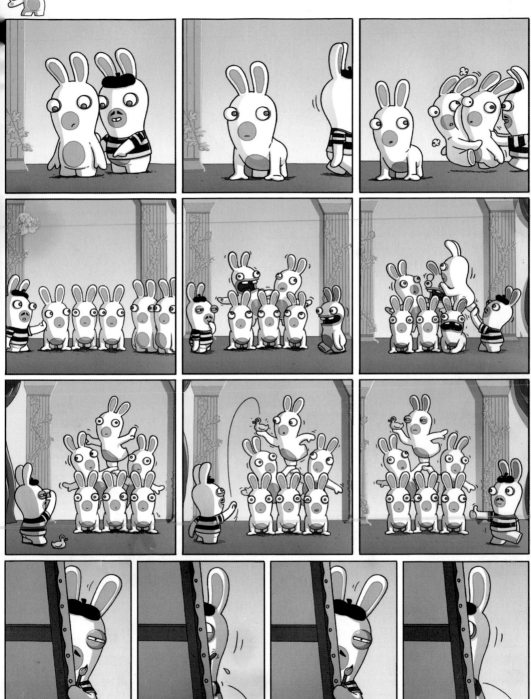

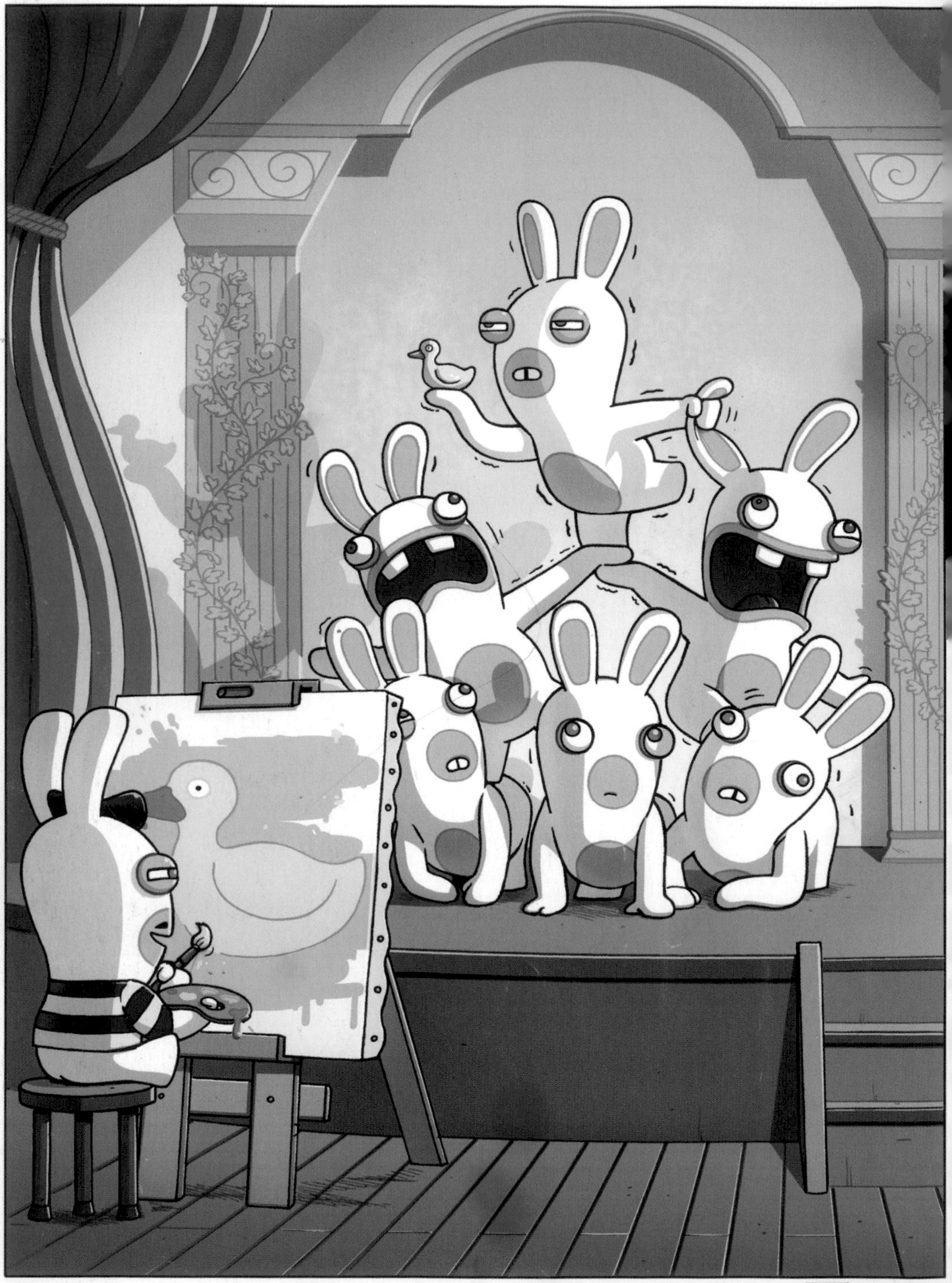
THITAUME -PUJOL-

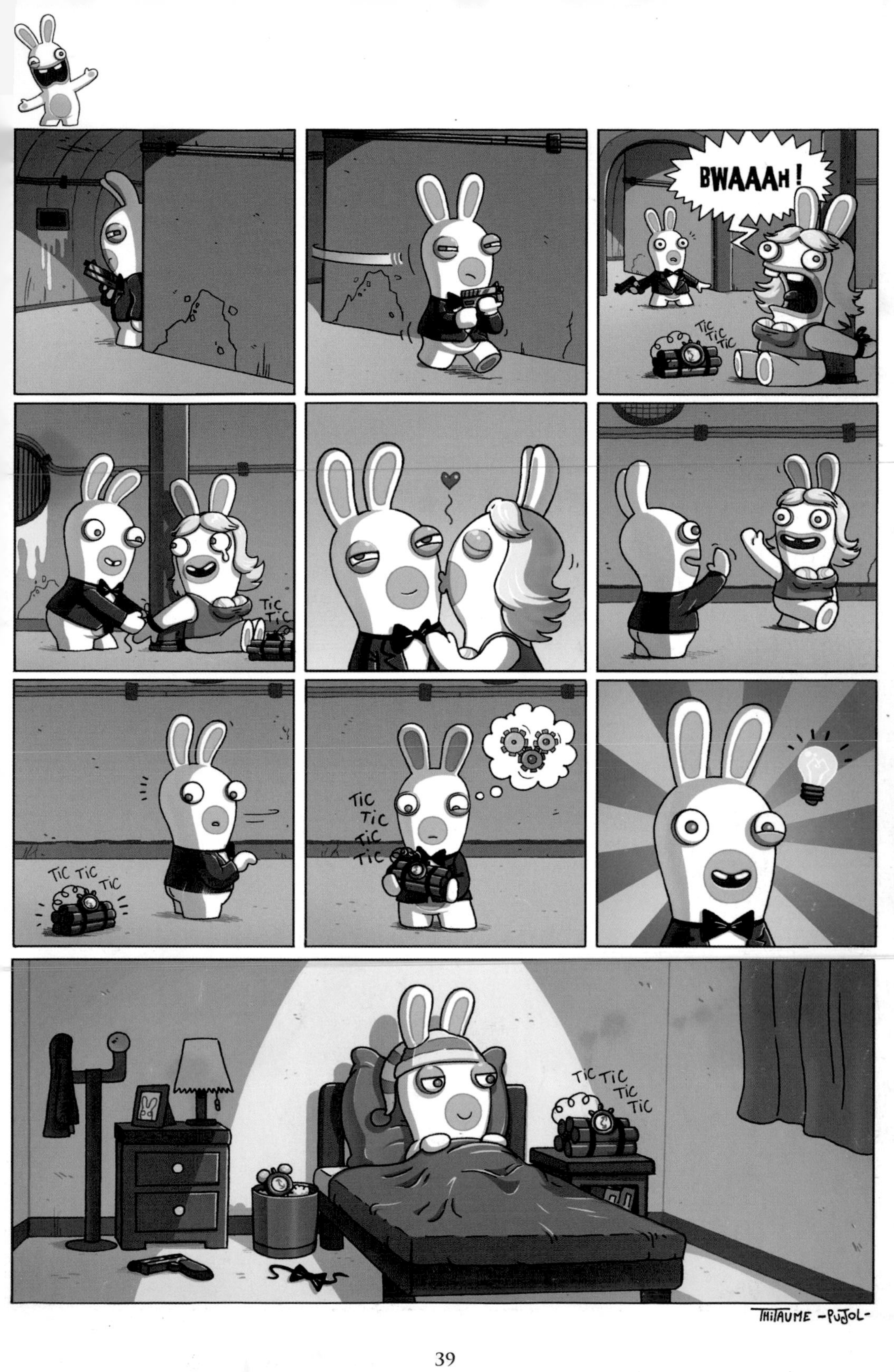
BWAAAH !
TIC TIC TIC
TIC TIC
TIC TIC TIC
TIC TIC TIC TIC
TIC TIC TIC TIC
THITAUME -PUJOL-

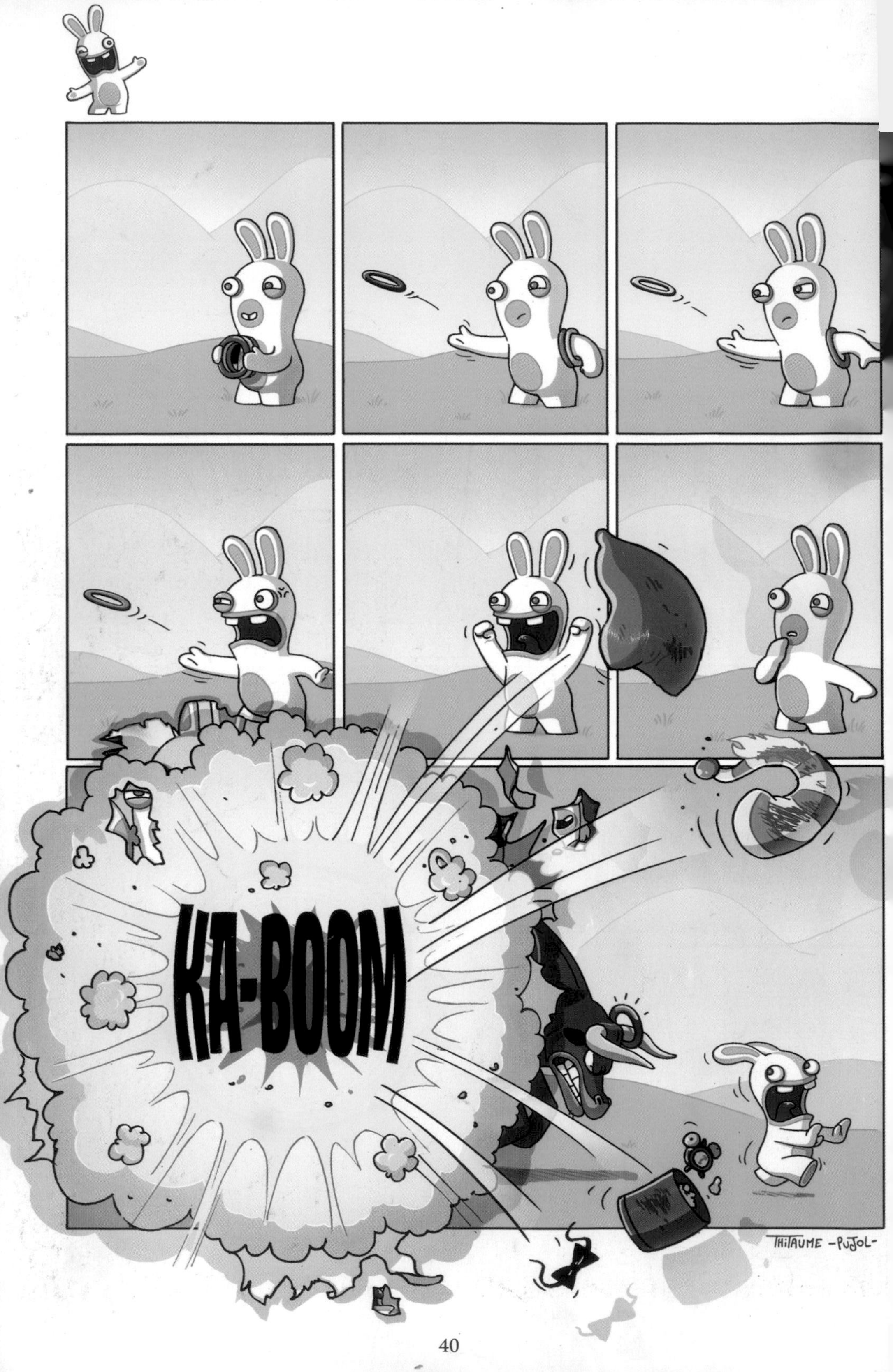
KA-BOOM
THITAUME -PUJOL-

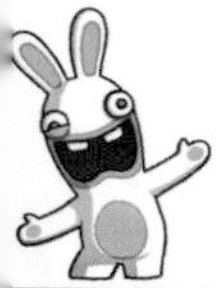

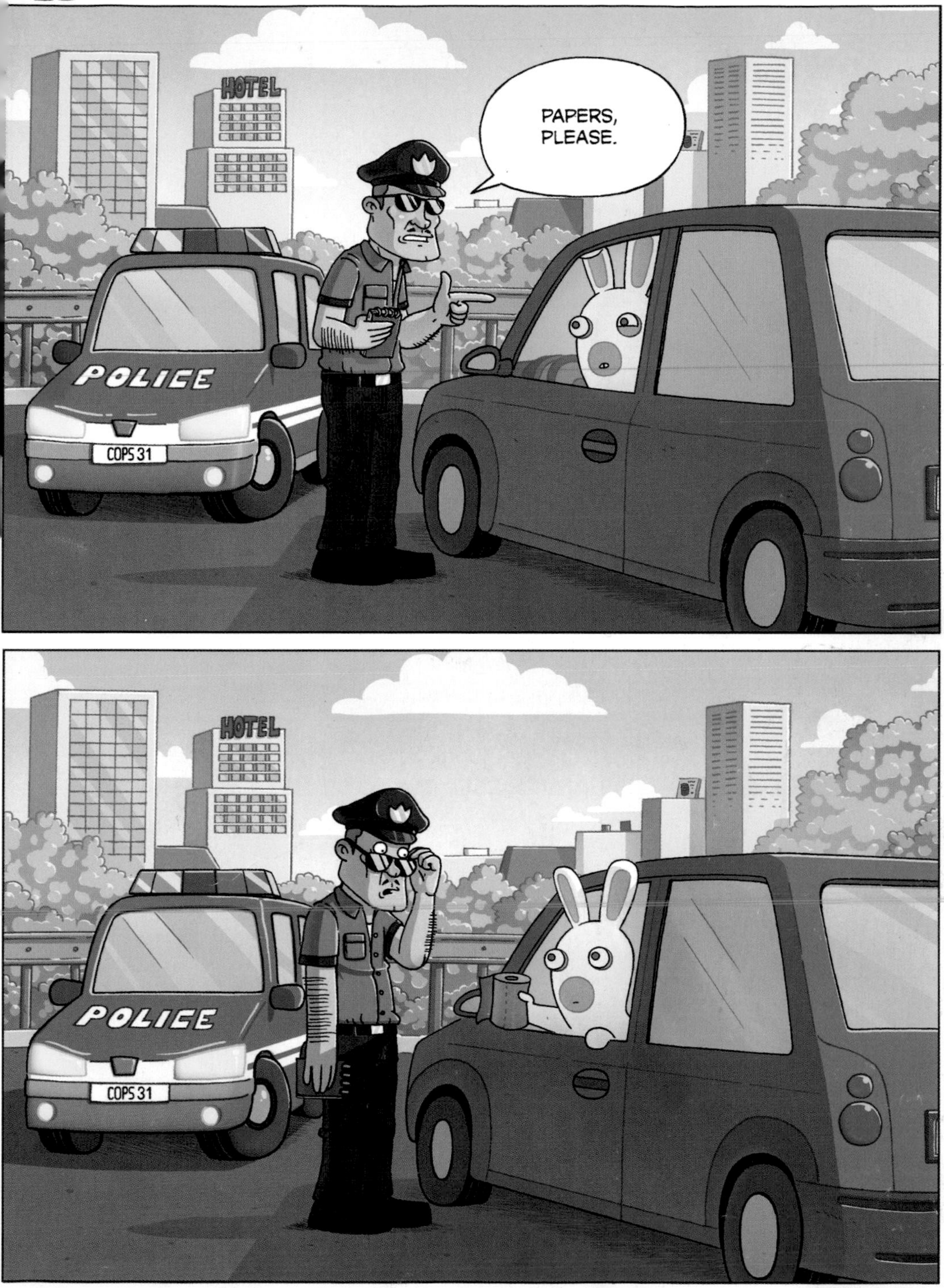
HOTEL
PAPERS, PLEASE.
POLICE
COPS 31
HOTEL
POLICE
COPS 31

THITAUME -PUJOL-

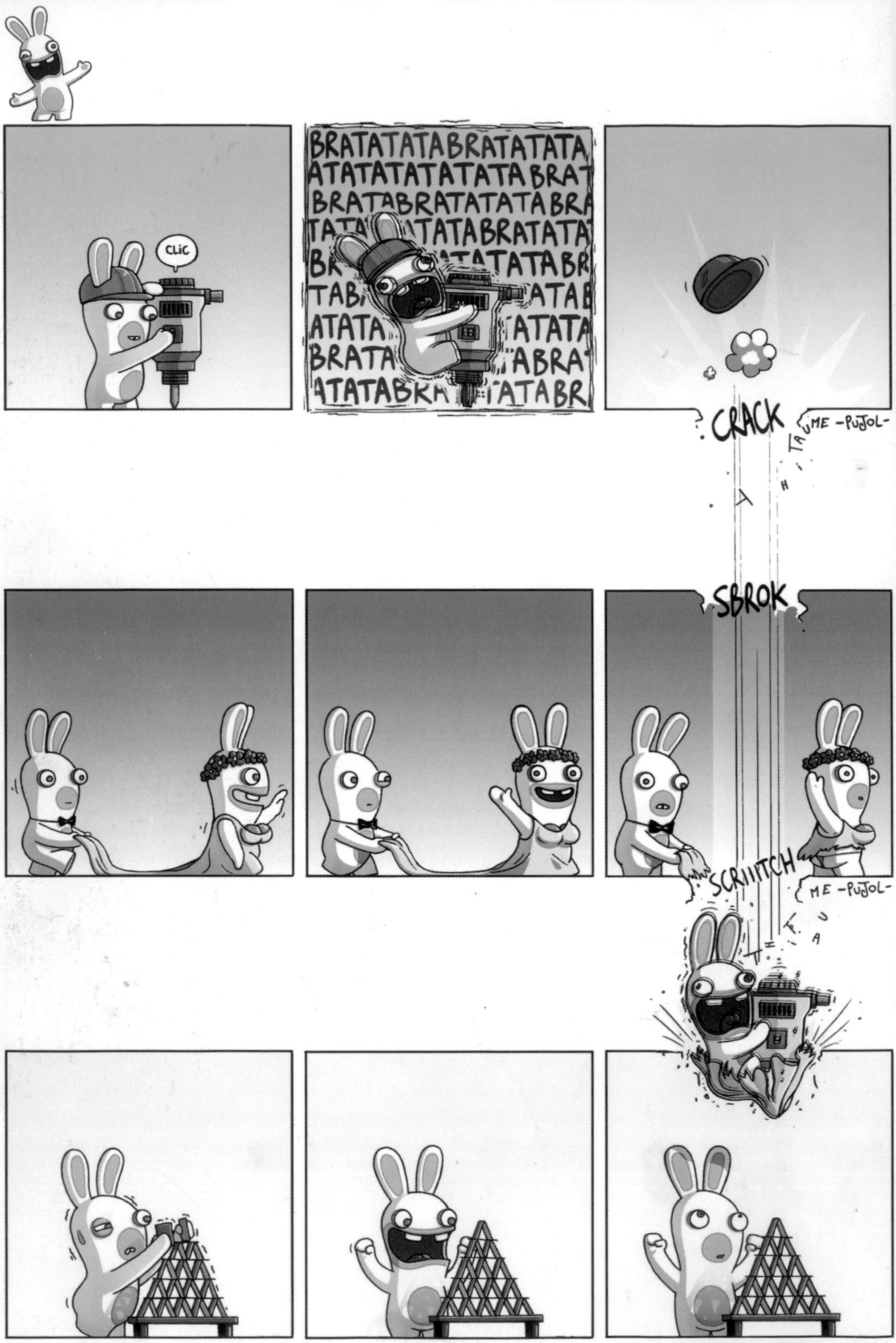
CLIC
BRATATATA BRATATATA
CRACK
THITAUME -PUJOL-
SBROK
SCRIIITCH
THITAUME -PUJOL-
THITAUME -PUJOL-

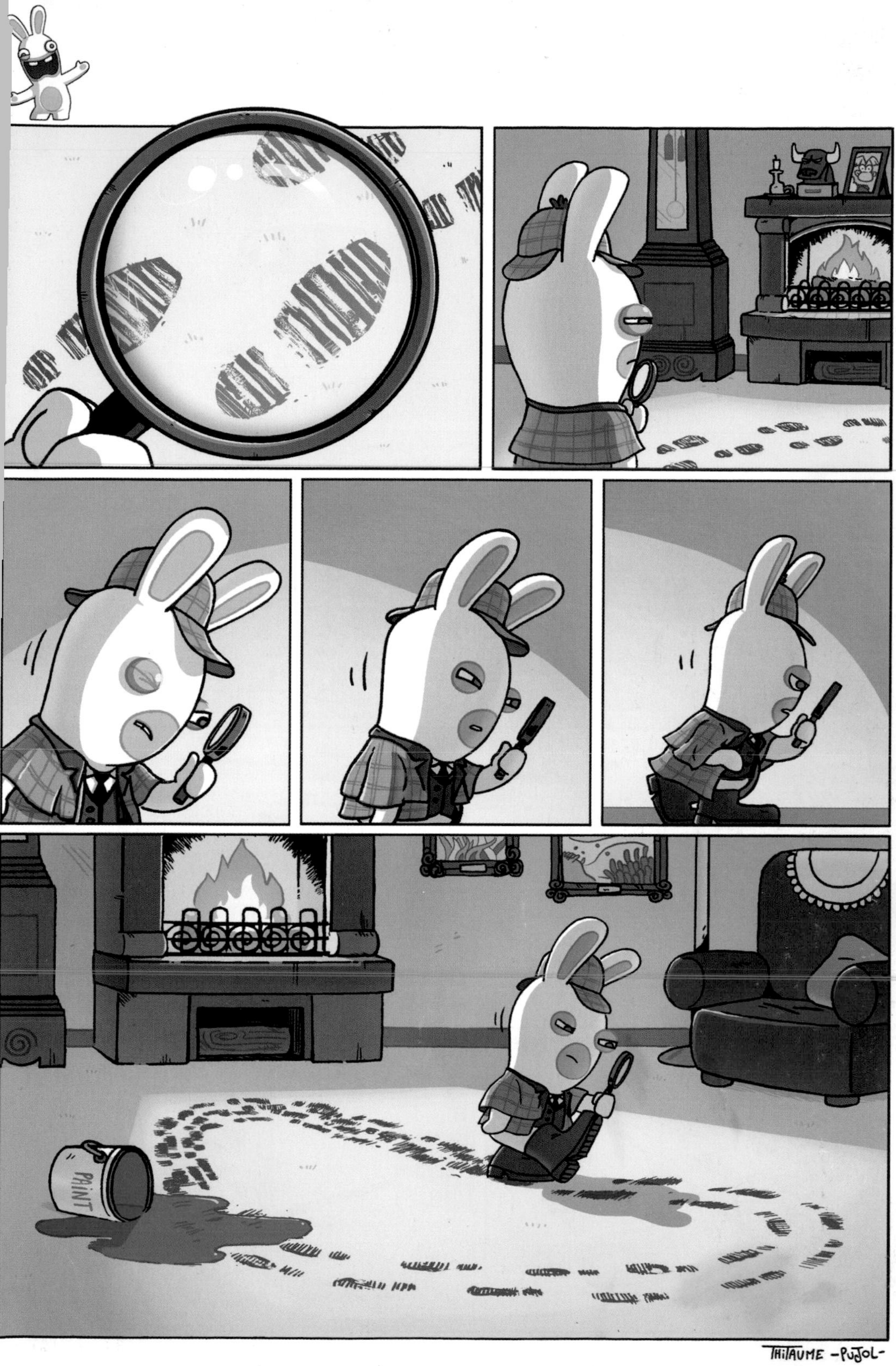
PAINT
THITAUME -PUJOL-

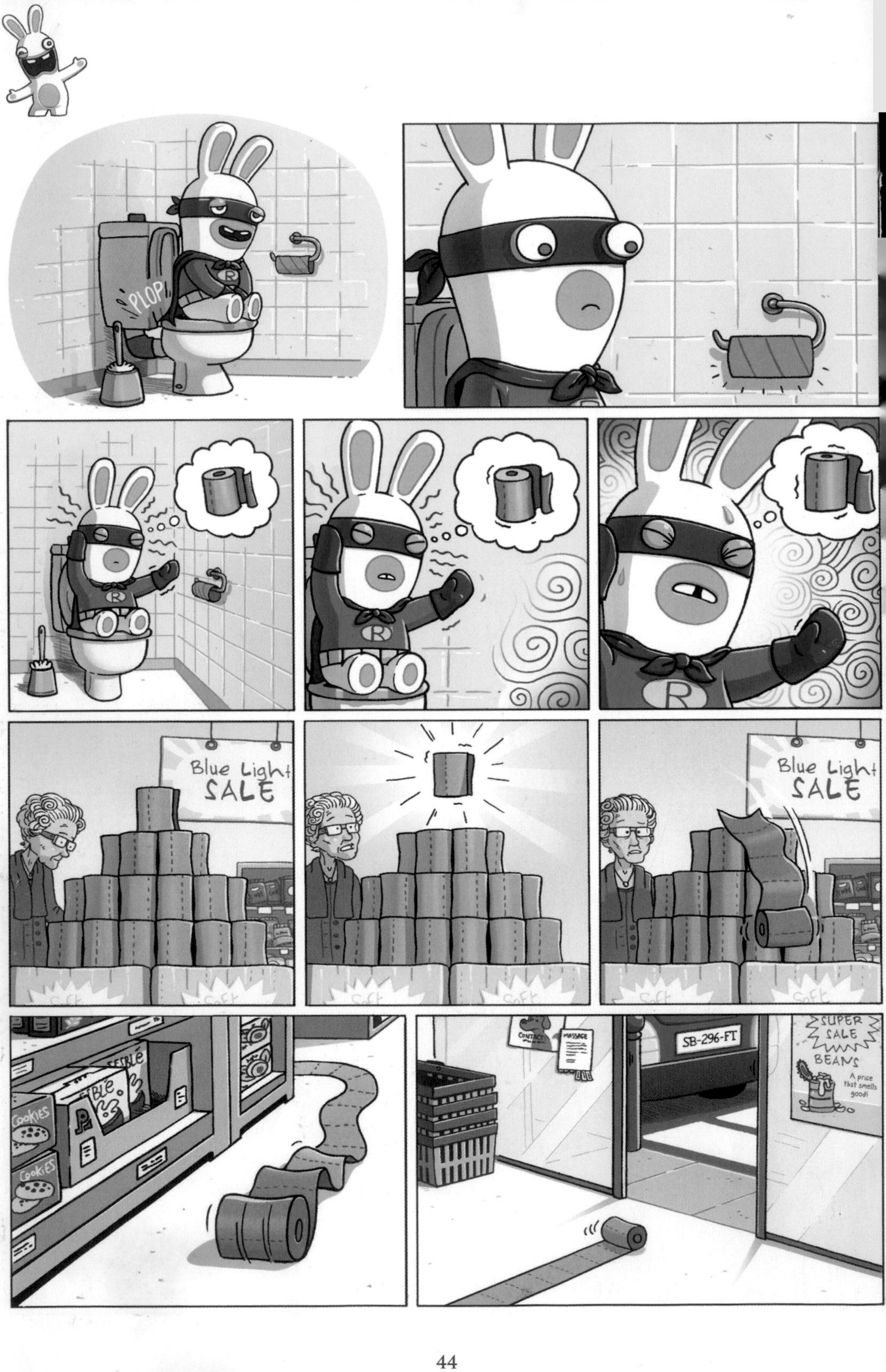
PLOP
Blue Light SALE
Blue Light SALE
COOKIES
COOKIES
CONTACT
MASSAGE
SB-296-FT
SUPER SALE
BEANS
A price that smells good!

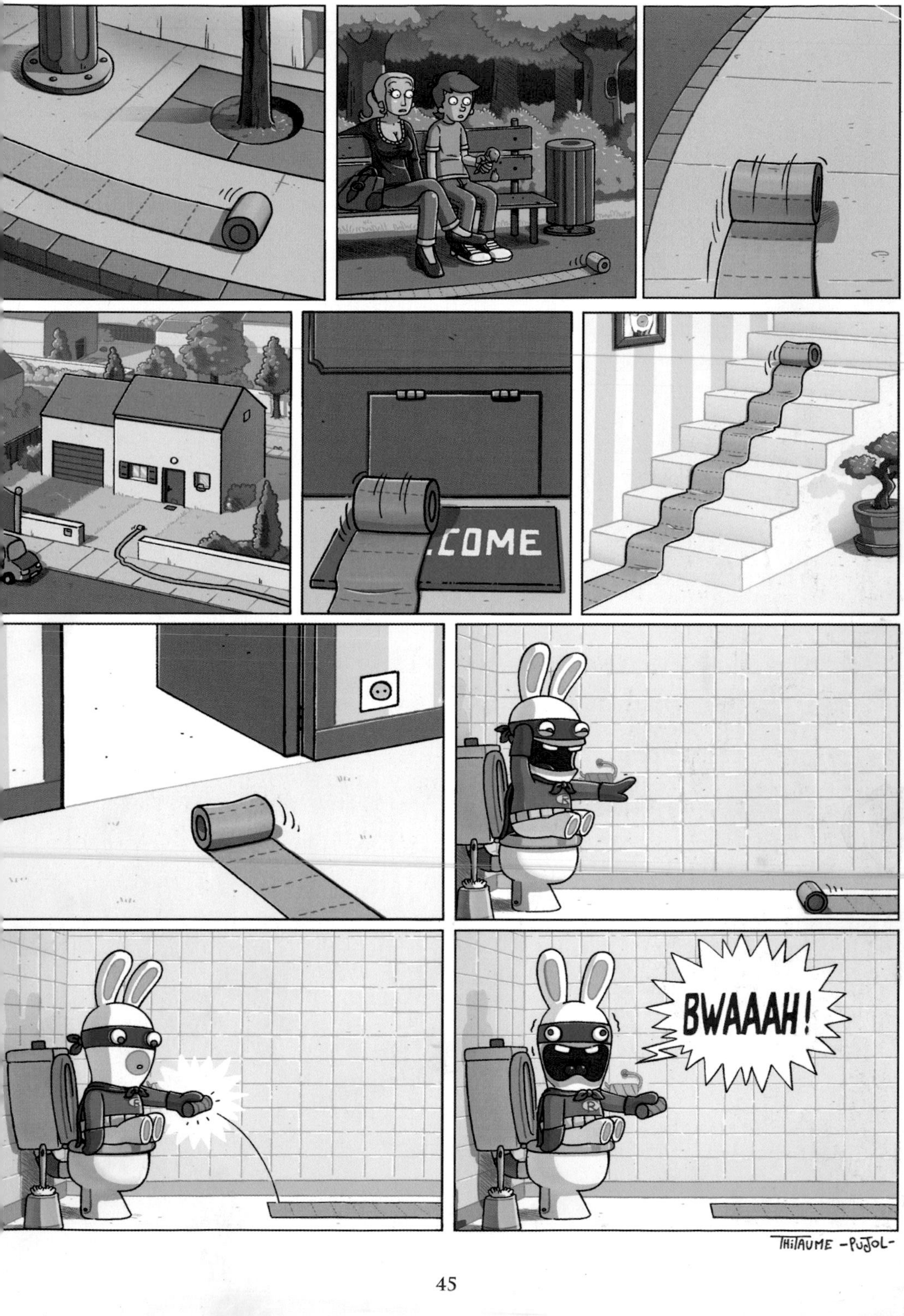
.COME
BWAAAH!
THiTAUME -PUJOL-

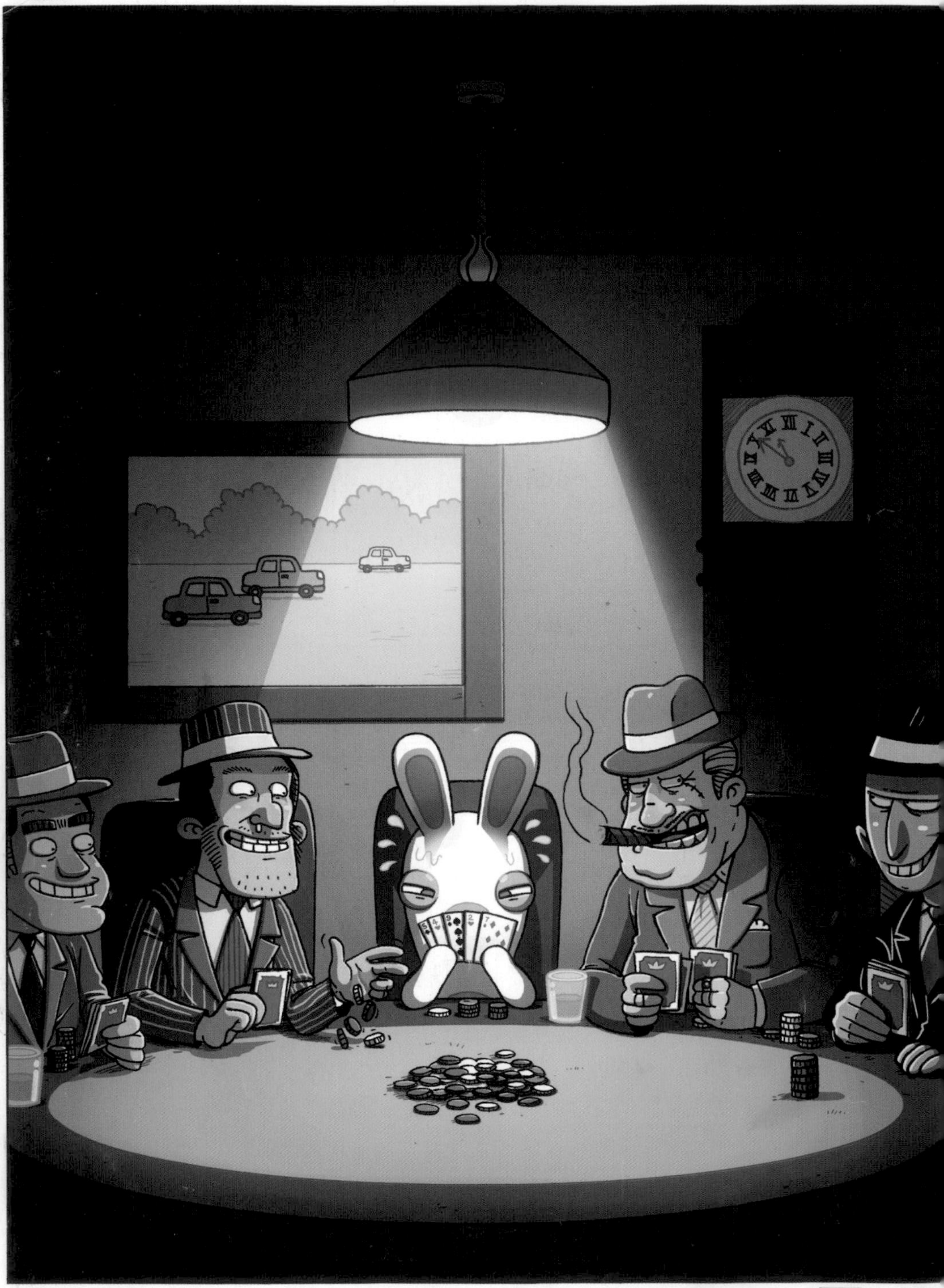

THiTAUME -PUJOL

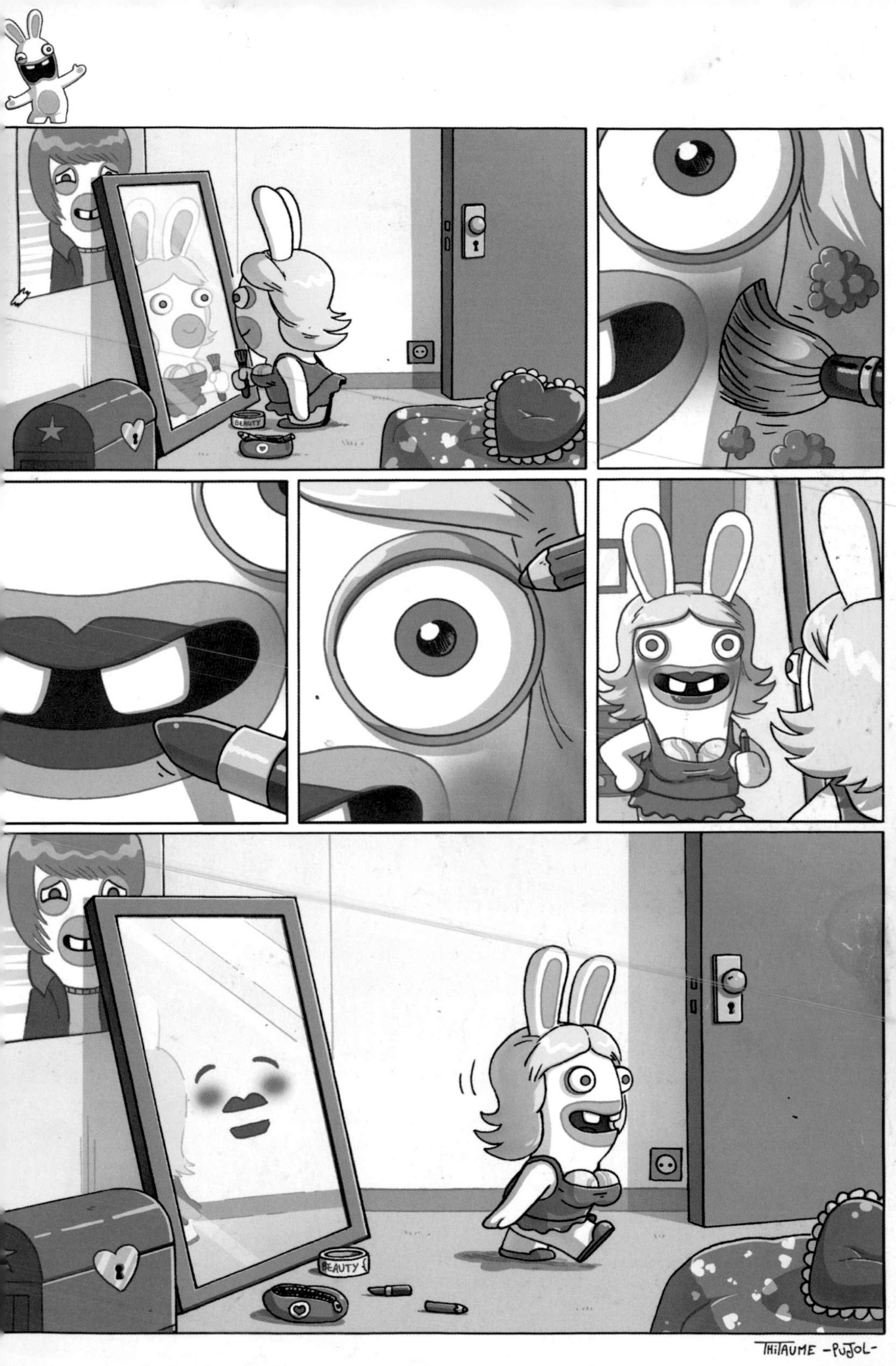

BEAUTY
BEAUTY
THILAUME -PUJOL-


The Rabbids return in an all-new full-length adventure in RABBIDS #2 Coming Soon!

# GOOD JOB!

## You're Almost There!

Now, go to page 4 and start reading!

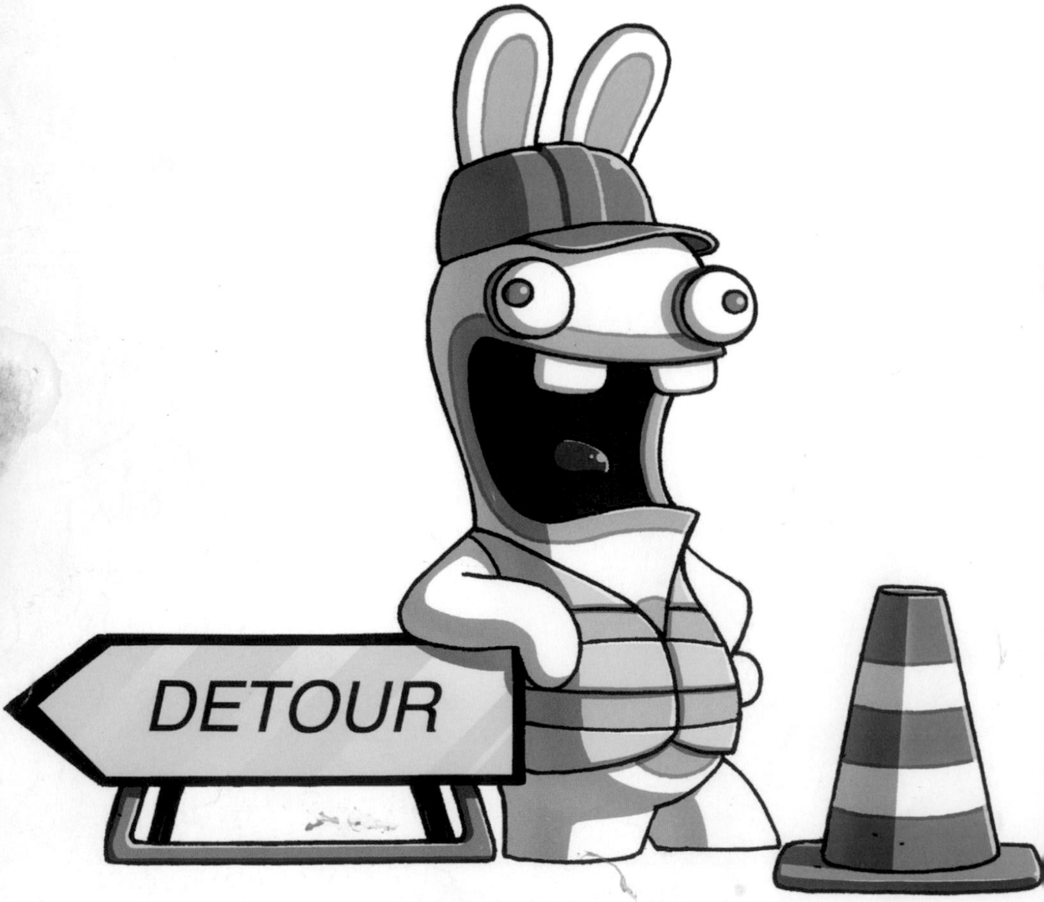
DETOUR

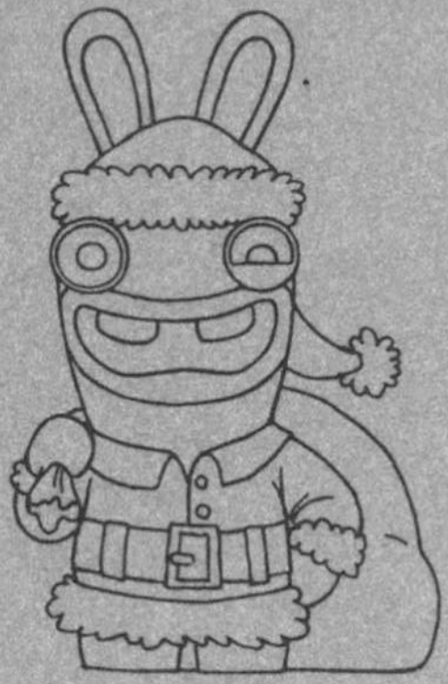
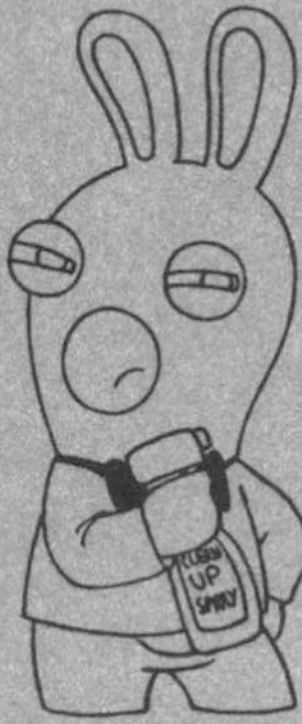
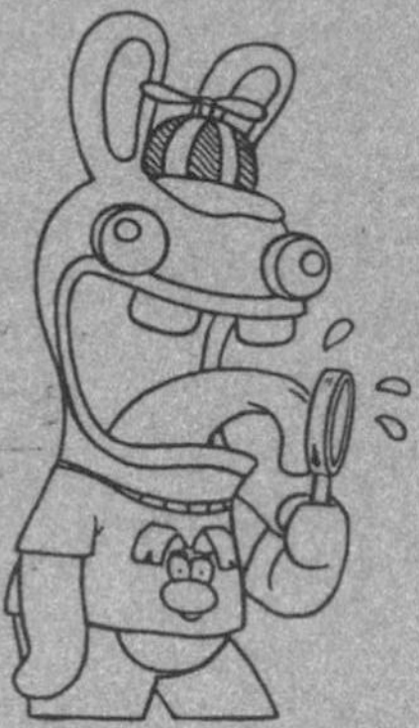
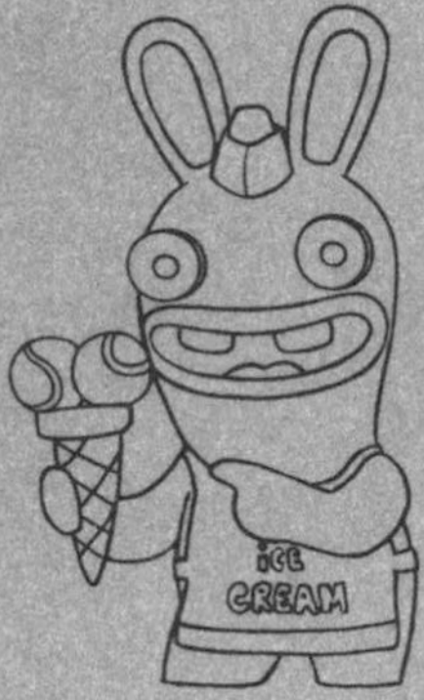
ICE CREAM
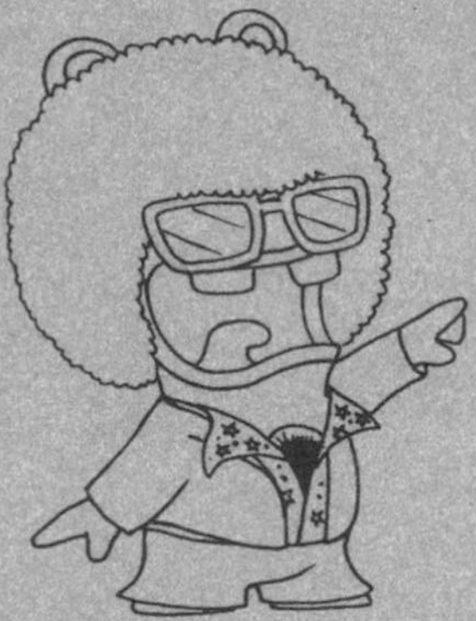
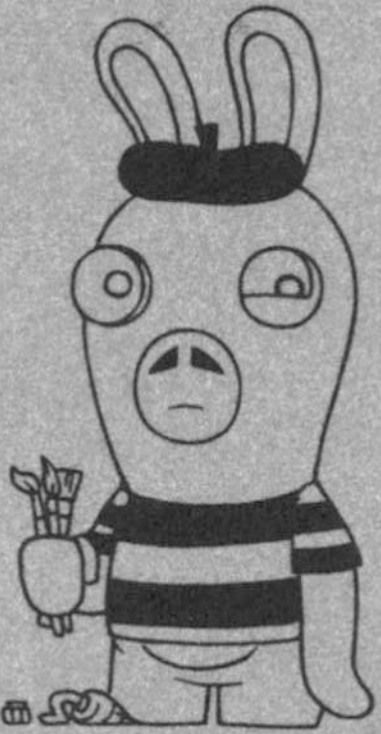
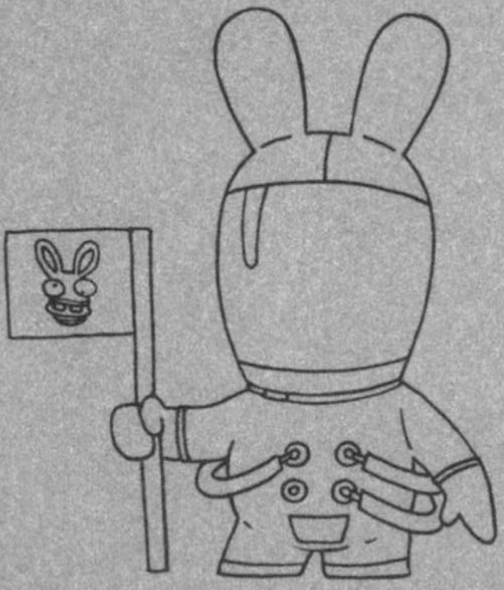
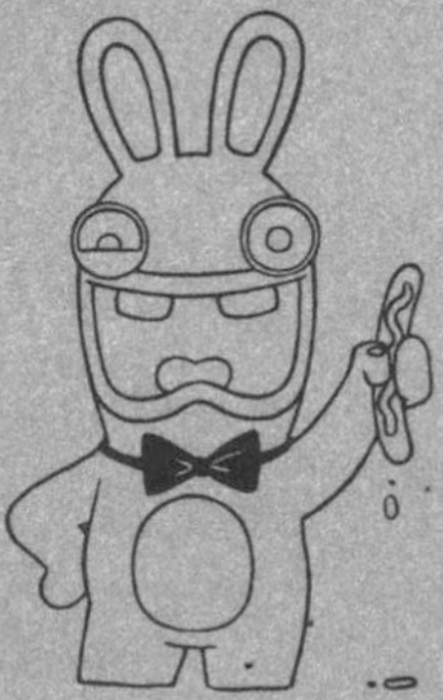
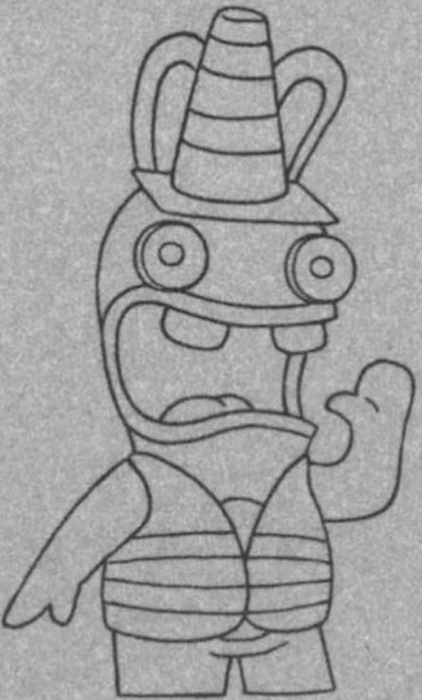

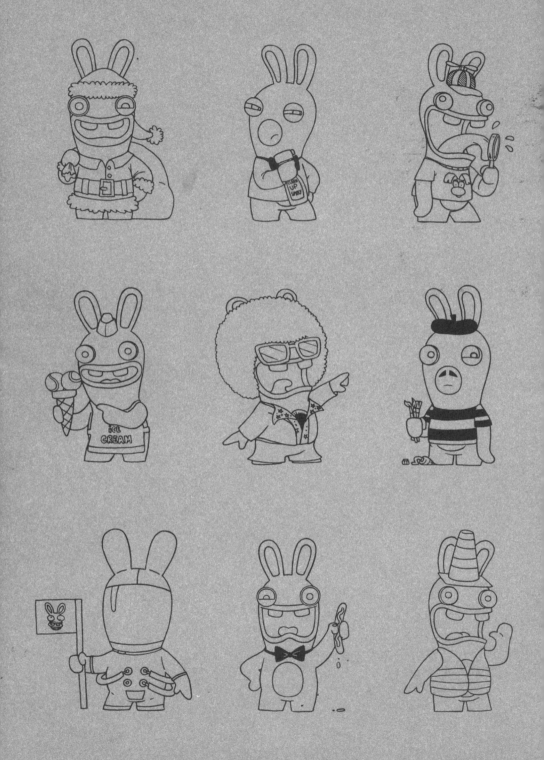